I0613307

Freedom's Price
Task Force 125, Book #5

Lisa Pietsch

Table of Contents

Copyright

Published by Defiance Press & Publishing, LLC

Bulk orders of this book may be obtained by contacting Defiance Press & Publishing, LLC. www.defiancepress.com.

Defiance Press & Publishing, LLC

281-581-9300

info@defiancepress.com

Task Force 125 Series

From The Path to Freedom, Chapter 18:

Brian had brown hair, dark brown eyes and a phenomenal tan. He was lean, long legged and seemed like he belonged on an Italian soccer team. His father served as a Navy SEAL in Vietnam and was still MIA. Brian fought his demons by also becoming a SEAL. When an operation went sour and the other members of his team were killed in action, he was recruited as an original member of Task Force 125 for his expertise in explosives. He lived hard. His motto was "Live fast, die young and leave a good looking corpse." He was a man who liked hard liquor, lots of women and risky work. When he wasn't on the job, he was either in or near water. He gave the term "frogman" a whole new meaning.

Chapter 1

Thick cloud cover inked out the sliver of a moon and added an eerie aura to deck of the aircraft carrier. Lieutenant Brian Allen popped a piece of gum in his mouth as he walked the staging area of the deck and surveyed the hustle around him. He listened as his SEAL team and their Royal Marine allies clicked magazines of ammunition into their weapons and completed function checks. He breathed in the salty Arabian Sea air as he embraced the pre-mission anticipation building inside him.

I love the smell of jet fuel in the morning.

The smell of jet fuel wafted across the deck as the Sikorsky helicopter's engine fired up. Their pilot began his preflight prep as the teams readied for combat. Bathed in the blue and green deck lights, the chopper had an otherworldly glow. She appeared as a dragon, a huge beast of war and destruction. Tonight's operation wasn't so much destruction as it was preventing it, though a small body count was expected for the Iraqis. The allies' mission was to land at the Al Basrah offshore oil terminal and take it before the retreating Iraqis blew it up. It was standard procedure for Saddam to order oil resources destroyed before the allies could capture them. If it was already rigged to blow, it would be Brian's team's job to disable the explosives and see that it didn't.

Brian patted the Sig Sauer handgun in his thigh holster and chambered a round in his M4A1 Carbine before looking at the faces of each of his four SEAL Fire Team members. "Ready to party?"

They shouted the affirmative "Hooah!"

Brian glanced over at his Royal Marine counterpart, a six-foot- three red-headed Scot who was built like a tank and could probably do as much damage. "Ready, Martin?"

Martin's green eyes sparkled as the blue and green deck lights reflected off the black greasepaint covering his face, giving him an almost serpentine quality. "Aye." Martin glanced at each of his four men in turn, apparently doing his own visual inspection. "Right, lads! Kit muster time is over. Lock and load!"

"Mount up, ladies! SEALs port, Marines starboard."

Their teams loaded into the open sided chopper, four men to each side, with their legs hanging out, ready to jump onto the deck of the oil terminal when the helicopter landed on it.

Brian and Martin climbed in last.

Whomp. The engine revved louder and the huge rotors began to spin slowly. *Whomp. Whomp.*

Brian's heart began to beat in time with the rotors as it always did before a mission. Something felt off tonight but he chalked it up to the enchiladas he'd had for dinner.

Whomp-whomp-whomp.

He breathed deep as the rotors spun the salty sea air around them and his blood raced. He lived for the adrenaline rush that missions brought with them. He was no different than the others.

Most of the men in special ops were adrenaline junkies and it suited them fine that way.

His breath quickened as the rotors worked up to their flying speed and a thrill raced through him as the bird lifted off the deck.

The men, packed in shoulder to shoulder inside, swayed with the chopper as it hovered over the deck for a moment, turned slowly, and then shot off at one-hundred-sixty miles per hour, flying low and fast, sandwiched between dark skies and deadly ocean.

They arrived at the oil platform in just minutes. The Sikorsky's nose pulled up for a quick stop where they'd planned for her to land and then take off again in seconds.

Brian tensed for the landing. "Ready, boys? Hop and pop."

"Hold up, LT!" The pilot turned to Brian. "We can't land. You're gonna have to jump it."

I could plan an operation for weeks, but nothing ever goes as planned.

These things happened, and Brian trusted the pilots he worked with. "Fast rope down?"

"Negative, sir. They've got c-wire about eighteen inches deep all over the deck. The rotor downwash could whip the rope and we'd get tangled. I'll hover as low as I can so you can jump from the skids."

Shit. Concertina wire, that spiral wire with razors attached to it every few inches. Great if you're behind it but you're guaranteed to bleed if you have to go through it.

Brian tensed his jaw and ground his teeth. He turned and grabbed Martin's huge shoulder before yelling into his ear so as to be heard over the whine of the engine and the thunder of the rotors. "C-wire on the deck. Gotta jump from the skids."

Martin nodded. "Right." Martin raised his voice so his men could hear him. "Oy, lads! Intel cocked up the recce. The LZ is laid with C-wire so it's time to go ninja!"

The men were all grunts and head nods. Going ninja was what they lived for.

Brian grinned. No matter what part of the world they came from, special forces troops all spoke the same language.

Martin hung on to the handle of the open side door and stepped onto the skid as the chopper lowered slowly over the woven mess of bloodthirsty wire. "Step lively, lads!"

Pride swelled in Brian for having the privilege of working with these men. Martin was a true leader by leading from the front and jumping in first. They'd all get tangled and chewed up in the wire and have some scars for it. As the first man in, Martin would take the brunt of the damage. With any luck they'd all live to tell the tale.

The pilot hovered the SeaHawk about seven feet above the platform.

The warm Arabian sea below the oil platform ebbed and flowed with its constant rhythm, filling Brian's lungs with the salty sear air he loved so much. Flashes of childhood summers on the beaches of Aqaba left his mind as quickly as they'd entered as shots rang out from below and Brian's training kicked in. "Deploy! Deploy! Hot LZ! Everybody out so we can get this chopper out of here!"

The Royal Marines and Brian's Navy SEALs jumped from the chopper like it was on fire.

Brian landed hard and crouched low in the concertina wire as the chopper cut away at top speed to avoid the barrage of bullets zinging toward it. The chopper's downdraft pushed the wire around the platform and into the men. Brian clenched his jaw and cursed at the sharp razors that dug into his calves but stayed low to avoid the enemy fire as he returned it.

We're surrounded. Somehow they knew we were coming.

His stomach tightened and heart beat loudly in his ears as he scanned the platform for the enemy shooters.

The Brits were tangled in the wire, but still moving slowly through it toward the outer perimeter of the platform where the Iraqis were lying low and raining down bullets on the two allied teams.

"Stay low!" Brian shouted as he returned fire. His and Martin's teams were completely surrounded, and the only way out was to shoot through hot lead.

"Bristol's down! Bulldog, watch your nine!" Martin was picking off as many of the Republican Guard as he could, but the allies were out manned and out gunned.

The rat-tat-tat of MP-5s slowed and Brian's heart rate shot up.

There should be more of our gunfire. Christ, I have men down!

The sharp, metal razors attached to the spiral bound wire grabbed at Brian's boots, tore at his trousers and sliced through the flesh on his calves as the Iraqis took shots at him and his team from all around the platform.

One of his men shouted gruffly from behind Brian. "Fuck! We're sitting ducks here, LT!"

Brian yelled over his shoulder. "Just stay low and lay it down, Wayne!" He turned to see where the rest of his SEALs were on the platform.

Davis is missing.

"Davis, status?" He shouted.

"Shit! Davis is down, LT!"

Brian's blood went cold. He looked over to where Davis should have been. Spencer crouched over him. "He's gone."

Fuck!

If they didn't want to be dead meatballs in this metallic spaghetti, they'd need to lay down a whole lot more fire.

Brian heard shots whizzing by and welcomed the music.

You never hear the one that kills you.

To his left, he saw one of his men crumple into the wire.

No, damnit!

Rage boiled inside him as Brian pinpointed the source of the shot and opened fire on three Republican Guards hunkered together. He knew they were dead when their guns stopped firing. He targeted the next source of gunfire and lay down a rain of bullets until his magazine was empty.

Reload. Silence.

Time to disarm the explosives the Republican Guards must certainly have set since they knew the allies were coming. "Martin, status?"

"Lost three. I've got one and me, LT. You?"

Brian turned to check on his men so they could regroup and move to their objective.

Four black clad SEAL bodies lay akimbo in the c-wire. "Jesus! Fuck!"

Brian gasped as he woke from the familiar dream. Sweat washed over his face and chest and the breeze from the air conditioner made it feel almost arctic in his luxury cabin on the yacht. He threw the sweaty bedding off himself and inhaled deeply, filling his lungs with the cool air that smelled of lavender air freshener rather than salty sea. He wiped the sweat from his face and ran his fingers through his wet hair.

Spy games with the CIA and living on a luxury yacht. I've come a long way in just a few years.

The new luxury yacht that served as the base of operations for American Swift was even better than the last but it couldn't sparkle enough to make the PTSD go away. He squeezed his eyes shut and ground his palms into his eyelids.

Good men gone and mourned by their families. Can I ever repay this debt I feel to them? Third time this week. Damnit. I need to see some action soon.

These were the ghosts driving Brian. Unless he was on a mission, unless he got that adrenaline fix, the flashbacks would continue to haunt him in his sleep. Post Traumatic Stress Disorder had a way of twisting every man's mind differently.

Sleep will be more and more difficult to come by unless I find an adrenaline fix soon. It's time I filed that transfer.

He walked to the bathroom, a private, marble encrusted shrine to the porcelain god. Stopping at the sink, he grasped the brushed nickel lever and pushed it back for some cold water. He splashed a few handfuls on his face and then dried off with the Ralph Lauren hand towel hanging nearby.

Too much luxury and too little reason for it.

He grabbed a file folder on his way out of the cabin and headed above deck to the office.

Chapter 2

Jennifer Santiago smiled her best "Please fund me?" smile into the webcam as she watched the faces of her investors on her laptop screen.

Blue-haired Beatrice Bertrand, the grand dame of the trust that had funded her marine archaeology work for the past five years, spoke. "Doctor Santiago, we were very impressed with your last project. The report and your subsequent publications met with high praise throughout the community."

Jennifer smiled graciously.

Not impressed enough to nominate me for the Keith Muckelroy Award, but that's okay. What I've got this time will knock everyone's socks off. What? Can you call me on Google Chrome? Hell yeah.

"We've enjoyed working with you for several years now and your research and projections have never come up short. If you say you can resurrect the remains of a Roman longship off the coast of Algiers, proving the existence of pirates during the time of the Roman Empire on this budget, then I believe I speak for all of us when I say, you have our full financial support."

Yes!

A wave of relief rushed through her and she relaxed a little. She didn't need to force the smile, it was just there.

The other investors nodded in their respective small squares on the screen.

Excitement bubbled inside her. "Thank you, Mrs. Bertrand. Thank you all. You won't be disappointed."

This will make me. I won't have to put up with any more of those stupid Lara Croft jokes at cocktail parties. I'll be able to write my own ticket after I bring this in!

"We never are, my dear." Mrs. Bertrand voice softened slightly. "I must bring up the issue of your work off the coast of Algiers though. It may sound insensitive, but the funding we're providing and the area of the world you'll be working in demands that we take out a K&R policy on you."

The happy bubbles of excitement popped.

They'd never taken out kidnap and ransom insurance on me before. On the one hand, it's high praise, but on the other, well, nobody hates kidnapping more than someone who's been kidnapped.

"Of course." Jennifer nodded soberly. She'd been kidnapped once before, but not for ransom.

She'd once thought following in her father's footsteps was a good idea so she applied for and was accepted into the Central Intelligence Agency's training program. During her final weeks on The Farm, Mike Spencer, one of the training officers, felt she needed some extra training in torture, more specifically, in being tortured and assaulted.

Her skin crawled and shoulders ached at the memory. She shook it off with a deep breath and a practiced smile. "Unless there's anything else, I'll get to work here while I wait for the paperwork and wire transfer. I can have a team assembled in a week."

"Wonderful! I'll have my secretary email you the paperwork in the morning. Congratulations, Jennifer. We're all very excited about this."

"So am I. Thank you again." Jennifer switched off the conference and closed her laptop. She knew being kidnapped was always a risk, but she checked in daily with her father whenever she travelled.

This is going to be the adventure of a lifetime!

~~~

Brian stepped out onto the sunny deck of the yacht American Swift was using as its base of operations. Docked in the Port of Tanger, it always had a beautiful view from sunrise to sunset.

Jason was already drinking coffee and watching TV on deck. "Morning, Bri. Dodgers beat the Mets."

"Brian, what is this?" Will Adams shook a fistful of papers as he stepped out of the main salon. "You put in for a transfer?"

The harsh tone in his voice startled Brian. Will had been a corpsman and seen his share of battle and blood, so nothing ever shook him. He had always been the calm one on the team. Will was Mr. Cool with ice blue eyes and dark brown hair, just a touch of grey at the temples, always perfectly in place, and his fitted, silk shirts and suits were never wrinkled. He was the man in charge now that Vince was in Russia, and always had an entire alphabet's worth of contingency plans. His eyes were dark today.

One thing he didn't like was when someone threw a monkey wrench into the plan, and that's just what Brian had done with his transfer request.

This isn't going to be pretty.

"Oh, hey, I wanted to talk to you about that. I haven't sent it yet." Brian reached for the file in Will's hand, but Will gripped it tight and chose to punctuate with it instead.

"We're a team, Brian. Why?" Will pointed the papers at him. "What's going on with you?"

Brian's stomach tightened. This was not the way he'd wanted to start this discussion. He shook his head.

I just had to put the file down on the counter and leave it there while I made coffee. Of course the coffee was so good I forgot the file there. Shit.

He hated the feeling of bailing on his team. These men were his brothers.

Time to face facts.

"Look, bro. Vince is gone. Sarah and Jay don't need us. You, me, Jason and Chris are just sitting on our thumbs while the rest of the world keeps on spinning. I can't just sit around. I need action."

Jason clicked off the TV and turned toward Brian. "Bri, we're a team. We're family." He sounded more confused than hurt. Jason had been the American Swift team's weapons specialist since its inception. The confusion on his face was like a dark shadow over the morning. This man was a bona fide badass, the kind of guy who storms a compound of heavily armed hostiles with a knife and kills them all like the grim reaper himself. But Jason had a pure heart. His friends, his team, were his world, and he'd destroy anyone who threatened them. This conversation was going to do just that and, Brian knew he needed to tread carefully.

Will turned toward Jason. "Unless I'm mistaken, these are transfer papers."

Jason scowled at Brian. "We go back a while. You were just gonna bail on us?" There was an edge to his question that cut through Brian.

Dana and Vince were the only original members who weren't still with the team. Vince was playing house in Moscow with the sister of a high-ranking Russian mobster. They were even expecting a baby. Dana, on the other hand, didn't find her happily ever after. She fell in love with her first mark, and that's bad business for a honey pot. Their mark, the guy she fell for, was a drug lord and he tossed her out of a helicopter for her trouble. Sarah Stevens had replaced Dana and surprised the hell out of the entire team. She and Jay were now undercover running smuggling routes between Russia, the Middle East, and Morocco.

"Guys, PTSD is kicking my ass. I need to do something now. I'll be around for the next assignment, but I need something to break up this monotony. I'm just requesting a side job, something to pick up the slack."

Jason smiled and eyed Brian. "A side job?" His voice rose as he asked the question. This particular smile was manic, and Brian knew trouble when he saw it.

Here it comes.

"What? Like a fisherman?" Jason stood and walked toward Brian. "Like a pizza delivery guy?" He tapped his head with both hands as though he'd had a breakthrough. "Oh, a waiter! You're gonna wait tables up at the casbah?" He stood in front of Brian and eyed him hard before lowering his voice to that very serious volume just above a whisper. "What the fuck sort of side job does a mutherfucking super-spy, navy SEAL, demolitions expert take?" Jason looked like a dog about to pounce. "Fuck no, man! This is it." He spread his arms out at the trappings of the luxury yacht. "You bite the bullet, live on this multi-million dollar yacht, wear your designer clothes, swim in the warm blue Mediterranean waters with all the pretty fishies, bang international broads day and night, and fucking like it!"

If I can't make my sale soon, Jason's going to get seriously angry.

Will sighed as he attempted to diffuse a situation that could quickly go south given Jason's short fuse. "Jason."

Jason flicked his Zippo open and closed several times and snapped at Will. "What? The original Spartan here wants to put in for a transfer and ditch his team", he pointed at Will for punctuation, "and don't you pretend it's anything else, because the job is too easy? Who the fuck quits when the going gets easy?"

He had to say "quit"? He knows I hate that word.

Brian's loyalties to himself and his team twisted his stomach into knots. He wasn't going to get anywhere with these guys. He had known Jason would feel betrayed but thought he'd be able to explain the PTSD.

They'd been a team for a long time. They were family and Jason was hurt. Now wasn't the time. "Jason, please."

"Hey, I get the adrenaline rush, dude, I get off on it too, but seriously, why would you give up all this?"

How many times have I asked myself that? This is a life people dream about but I just want to get out in the field so I can have the sweet comfort of hearing bullets whistle by. I must be insane.

"It's a gilded cage, Jason. It's not my style."

Jason shook his head, walked back to his chair, and sat. "Fuck you, man. I've been in bamboo cages and gilded cages, and I'll tell you what, mutherfucker. I'll take a gilded cage any day of the week and twice on Sunday! We've earned this. Uncle Sam owes us this."

I know he's right, but I need sleep at night.

"I'm getting ragged, man. I can't sleep. When it's time to finally run an op, I won't be any good to you."

Jason looked down at the deck as he lit a cigarette. "Bullshit." He didn't look back up.

Brian knew Jason would have a hard time forgiving him, and it pulled at his gut to hurt a brother who had saved his ass more times than he could count, but he couldn't see any other way to get the adrenaline rush he needed to keep the flashbacks at bay.

Will broke the silence. "Let's not make any hasty decisions. Maybe we can get you into Moscow with Sarah and Jay? We need supplies before they get here and we sail out to deeper waters for debrief. Why don't you both cool off by putting all that energy to use constructively?"

Always the voice of reason. Maybe Will can find an answer we can all live with?

Jason rose from his seat and slapped Brian on the shoulder. "Yeah, and if you're still jonesing for some action, I'll kick your ass in the town square when we're done."

Brian eyed Will, who had successfully averted what could have been a bad breakup.

Will smiled and crossed his arms over his chest as he leaned back in his chair. One nod told Brian what had just happened.

You son of a bitch. You knew Jason would pull me back from sending in the paperwork today. You ran this whole scene like a boss.

"That could help." Brian shook his head and suppressed a grin at his own ability to underestimate his teammates.

"Please don't kill each other." Will sighed. "I don't need any more paperwork today. The supply list is inside on the bulletin board."

Chapter 3

Jennifer breezed down the dock to her yacht and down into her cabin feeling energized and optimistic after meeting with her investors. She finally had the financial go-ahead to start work on a once-in-a-lifetime dive.

She stopped short at the closed door when she heard noises inside.

Eeew! Somebody is having sex in my bed?! She steeled herself, then opened the door.

What she saw was far more than she'd bargained for and something she wished she could unsee. Her employee, Gary, was entertaining a lady.

Oh, dear God!

Jennifer gasped and stepped back, grasping for control of her stomach as it convulsed with the need to vomit.

Gary looked up at Jennifer through the woman's legs. "Hey, baby. I thought we could have a threesome."

You what? Oh my God, I think I'm going to lose my lunch!

His words shot the whole scene well beyond surreal.

I can't decide which is more revolting – having to see this or knowing I'll have to burn those Ralph Lauren sheets. Fuck my life.

Shocked and revolted, Jennifer scoffed. "I can't imagine what would put such a horrific idea in your head. You both need to get off my bed and out of my cabin. Lady, please stop what you're doing?"

"Okay, I'll be done in a minute and we'll take off."

"Now, Gary! You've been making one excuse after another to live on my boat, eat my food and sponge off me between jobs and I'm tired of it. I don't care how good a diver you are, you are not worth the expense or the hassle."

Gary sat up and the woman tumbled to the floor and shouted, "Hey!"

"Both of you need to get the hell off my boat now!"

Gary looked stricken. "Netta was almost done, baby."

Jennifer's stomach turned. How had she dealt with this man for this long? He was great as a marine archaeologist and had an excellent mind for the work, but he'd become the ultimate slob and just plain sleazy. Jen smiled and stepped toward Gary. She picked up his shirt from the floor and tossed it over his genitals. "Cover your shame, Gary. You're done. Just go."

"What?"

How can he still be confused?

"Get the fuck off my bed and get out! You can fish your shit out of the harbor." She snatched up the clothes on the floor and strode across the hall to his cabin, grabbing all his clothes in a great armful, as she bounded up the stairs and out onto the deck.

"Hey, that's my stuff!"

Go get it. You look like you need a bath anyway.

She tossed them overboard and then shouted down the stairs to her cabin. "Don't ever let me see your face again you motherless fuck or I'll ruin you." She stomped onto the bridge, ripped his laptop computer from the cord and cell phone from its charger, and threw them both out the window and into the crystal blue Mediterranean waters just as he ambled up the stairs to the deck.

"You cunt!" He was still naked, and in the bright light of day, grotesque.

Why do they always go to the "C" word?

"Yeah, right. I almost forgot." She grabbed the nearby flare gun off the wall. "Take your nasty little friend with you now before I finish you both with a gut full of burning phosphorous, you gross piece of shit."

"You don't want to do this, Jenny." He wagged a finger and grinned as though he knew something she didn't. "You'll regret it." He reached for her. "Come on, now. You're going to need me for your work in Algeria. They'll eat you alive out there."

The hell I will! You've been eating me out of house and home for months!

"And monkeys might fly out of my ass! I'll be just fine. I can find five more of you within twenty-four hours. By the way, I don't like being called Jenny. Now, get out."

His eyes narrowed as he cupped his crotch. "You're gonna miss this."

It's hard to miss something you never wanted in the first place, loser.

17

The best she could muster was disgust. "You may think that's a big deal, but you really should get checked. It could be the sign of more severe health issues."

"You bitch."

Oh, yeah, that hurt. Shut the hell up and stop stinking up my yacht.

Relief washed over her. She'd been looking for a good excuse to get rid of him for a while now. This incident, finding him in her bed - the pig didn't even have the decency to use his own bed for his afternoon fright - was all she needed to cut him loose. She'd have to do twice the work and train a new diver, but it would be worth it.

She looked around. People on boats in the neighboring slips were standing on their decks watching the commotion on hers.

Might as well give them a good show.

She glared at a couple of her yacht club neighbors who were pointing at her and laughing loudly. "What are you looking at? Mind your own business."

Gary put his shirt on and still didn't have any pants. "Jenny, put the gun down and take it down a notch. I'll send Netta home and we can discuss this like grownups. You're acting ridiculous."

"I'm ridiculous? You really have no idea how you look right now, do you?"

Let's see if he understands public humiliation and gets the hell off my boat.

She turned back toward Gary. He stood there looking lost with his mouth wide open and his hands cupping his genitals.

Why won't he just leave?

~~~

Brian hopped from the boat to the dock and stretched. They'd been out to sea for a few weeks while Sarah Stevens and Jay Stanstead had some tactical fun in Moscow, but the dynamic duo were flying into Morocco soon for a debrief and some downtime. The best place to do that was offshore, so this was the perfect time to refuel and resupply the yacht before they went back out to deeper waters. Brian envied Sarah and Jay the action they had been seeing, working undercover in Moscow with the Russian mob.

Brian laced his fingers together and stretched his arms in front of him as he looked up at Jason who was still on the yacht. "You putting on weight lately?"

"Yep. Dropped my bodyfat two percent though."

"How can an Army grunt like you put on muscle out to sea?"

Jason puffed up his chest. "Lots of bacon, brother. Lots of bacon."

Brian, a Navy SEAL before being recruited to the CIA, smiled. Jase was a rugged son of a bitch and a trump card whenever you needed a man to cover your six. "Whatever. Let's go."

Jason stood, stock still, a dazed look in his eyes as he stared past Brian without responding.

"Jase!" Brian followed the direction of Jason's gaze and stopped dead when his gaze made contact with the brunette on the deck of the yacht in the next slip. Brian let his eyes wander up every inch of her legs to the most epic ass he'd ever seen. He let out a low wolf whistle and shook his head as she went inside.

Jason mumbled a low "um-hmm" as he nodded in agreement. His eyes were wide when he finally spoke to Brian. "Damn, son! Did you see the ass on that?"

Brian nodded. "I'd like to see a lot more of the ass on that, so let's go restock so we can say hello to the goddess next door."

I'd like to do much more than just say "Hello".

Jason stepped onto the dock just as a very unattractive, naked woman jiggled up onto the deck next door. He recoiled. "What the...?"

Brian winced, turning away from the fright. "Sweet baby Jesus."

"It's like a train wreck." Jason cringed. "It's so horrific."

Brian watched as the hottie walked back up on the deck, followed by a fat man.

Jason said what Brian was thinking. "What the fuck kind of clown car is that boat?"

Through all the naked horror, Brian watched as the beautiful Latina in the tight skirt pulled out a flare gun.

Shit just got real.

Jason sidestepped closer to Brian "What a woman."

Brian now understood the gist of the story unfolding in the next slip. The guy, who was entirely too sloppy to have access to a fine piece of

Latina tail like that, had been busted getting his knob slobbered by the cottage cheese queen. Never had Brian seen anything so tragic for the male of the human species since Hugh Grant got busted with Divine Brown while Elizabeth Hurley waited for him at home.

Jason gasped. "Ooh! A flare gun!" He elbowed Brian as his face lit up like a kid at Christmas.

Nothing turns Jason on more than a woman who can wield a weapon and raise a little hell.

Brian watched as the naked woman flailed about in protest, whining about her clothes being lost. The Latina held the flare gun with both hands, her full breasts pushed together which amplified her generous cleavage as she aimed and told the naked chump and his five-dollar honey to get off her boat. Brian's lips curled into a smile.

I think I'm in love.

Jason was so enamored and excited he didn't bother to keep his voice down. "What a loser! Even I wouldn't touch that with a ten-foot pole. And that one," he pointed at the Latina. "I could get hard for her any time, even with a flare gun pointed at me. Shit, I've got a semi right now."

~~~

Jen glared over at him but couldn't for long. She chuckled at the playful grin and bright hazel eyes that gave her the impression this neighbor might very well be the life of happy hour where he came from. She stopped, mid-chuckle, as she made eye contact with the man standing next to him.

Mr. Semi was cute in a devilish sort of way, but the man standing next to him was all kinds of handsome and much more her type than any man she'd ever seen. His brown eyes met with hers and a thrill shot through her. She paused for a breath, turned back toward Gary and watched his mouth drop as the handsome man spoke.

"You'd better get off her boat, buddy. She's got a finger on that trigger and there's no shame as painful as burning phosphorous."

His deep, clear voice resonated somewhere deep inside her, both calming and exciting at the same time.

~~~

Brian smiled at the beautiful woman commanding the situation, then at the pathetic naked man.

You stupid bastard. You should be begging to stay. As it stands, you'd better move it on over because there's a line forming to be her next target.

She returned his smile, and despite the situation clearly being serious for her, he suspected she was holding back laughter too.

Lady, you are too beautiful and too fierce for a loser like that. You deserve a real man.

Hell, a real man wouldn't stray from a babe like that. He'd stay close and mark that territory with diamonds, pearls and every sparkly thing known to man. Brian blinked as he came back to reality, the nature of his thoughts surprised him. He had always prided himself on staying delightfully unattached while still having all the female companionship he could stand. This feeling? This was uncomfortable.

The naked man finally jumped in the drink for some clothes she'd thrown overboard while the naked woman stomped onto the dock and shouted in a deep, surprisingly masculine voice. "Get me some clothes, damnit!"

"Yeah, cover that shit up, man." Jason shouted as he started walking toward shore. "This is a high class yacht club."

The woman, eyes dark with liner that had smeared, stared at Jason and flashed a smile minus a few teeth. "Nice boat. You want to party?"

Sweet baby Jesus! That bitch is more frightening than Halloween!

Jason shivered, picking up his pace as he walked by.

Brian shook his head as he watched the beautiful Latina disappear below deck. He and Jason continued in silence to their Range Rover parked in the lot just past the slips.

Jason unlocked the range rover with a click of the fob just as they came into remote range. It was safer that way, just in case someone was smart enough to plant an explosive. "Did you see the rack on that broad? And the legs! I should go over and console her tonight. She wants me."

"Jase, that was no broad. That's a whole lotta woman, and I'll thank you to speak respectfully when referring to the future Mrs. Allen."

Jason choked on a chuckle and slapped Brian on the shoulder. "Yeah, right! You're the biggest whore dog east, north, south and west of the Pecos!"

Once upon a time, but not anymore.

"Not anymore." Brian walked to the passenger side of the Rover as Jason made for the driver's side. He stooped to retie his shoe, an excuse to look under the SUV and search for possible bombs. In their line of spy craft, they could never be too safe.

"The fuck you say?" Jason faked a stumble and dropped his keys under the truck to get a good look underneath. He grabbed the keys when he was done.

"I'm done whoring. I'm going to marry that woman."

They opened their doors, and as per procedure, discretely checked under their seats for anything out of the ordinary.

Jason stared across the seats at Brian. "You sound serious. Don't play like that."

I've never been more sure of anything else in my life. She's the one.

Brian smiled. "You'll see."

"I won't hold my breath." Jason chuckled to himself. "Hey, remember Ahmad?"

Brian stepped into the vehicle. "How could I forget? I was your spotter."

Ahmad had specialized in placing Bouncing Betty land mines under car seats of NATO commanders. His body count was downright impressive until some army grunt took him out in a parking garage with a 50 caliber sniper rifle. Brian grinned. Jason always was a crack shot.

"A damned good one too. That poor bastard dropped like a wet rag. He never saw it coming. Best way to go, if you ask me." Jason climbed into the driver's seat and started the engine.

"He had a beautiful signature though." Brian had to respect the bomb maker's work. Sun Tzu said "To know your Enemy, you must become your Enemy." And occasionally a bomb maker would live long enough that the demolitions experts tracking him developed a very personal relationship without ever meeting them. Ahmad had been a worthy opponent for Brian.

But that's all ancient history now. Things are about to change.

Chapter 4

Jennifer thanked the server for her drink and raised it to her lips.

Time to celebrate my funding and the fact that lazy ass Gary isn't on my payroll anymore.

She stopped mid sip as the tall, dark and handsome man from the boat in the slip next to hers walked into the yacht club lounge.

Hello, handsome!

She had been around enough divers to know a swimmer's body when she saw it. His chest was solid. He wore a freshly pressed shirt but his pecs were clearly defined. His shoulders were broad and well-muscled. Arms like steel cables finished in large, yet proportionate hands that were surprisingly well manicured.

Oh, God. Please be straight.

His legs were long and lean. She suspected they were probably topped with a delicious, tightly muscled ass. She took a shallow breath before sipping her drink and placing the glass back on the table.

I wonder if you've got rock-hard abs under that shirt?

She felt her cheeks burning with a nervous blush as she thought about it.

What's wrong with me? I meet lots of men and never have crazy thoughts like this! Oh, but he does take my breath away.

Jennifer turned and looked out the window beside her to give her blush a moment to cool.

He's probably some egomaniac with too much money and time on his hands.

She couldn't resist turning and watching as he sidled up to the bar and sat on one of the stools.

He moves like liquid.

She watched as he reached into his pocket and pulled out a shiny gold coin, twirling it over and under his long fingers as he waited for his drink.

Jennifer could hear her ovaries swoon and damned them for their easy betrayal.

God help me, I'd have his babies.

~~~

Brian felt a stare as he walked into the yacht club lounge. He turned to see the beautiful, hot-headed Latina he'd admired earlier.

She doesn't have her flare gun. This must be my lucky day!

A glance from her dark brown eyes both seared and beckoned.

He took a step to walk up to her but changed his mind and turned toward the bar instead.

Jesus! I've never been this nervous around a woman before. What the hell?

Confusion over whether or not to move in for the kill was not a feeling Brian was familiar with, and it was about as surprising to him as getting mugged. He pulled his gold coin from his pocket and rand it over and under the fingers on his left hand nervously.

Why does she make me feel like I'm in high school?

Her shoulder length, light brown hair shimmered with subtle highlights. Her bronze skin glowed and her brown eyes seemed to sparkle as she watched him.

Look at those legs! I've seen plenty of women in my time but, darlin', you are a vision.

She took his breath away, and he planned to return the favor— right after he had a drink. She met his gaze boldly. Something about her stare thrilled him.

This is no ordinary woman.

He smiled and watched as her full lips curved into a grin.

This is all wrong! After years of being a whore-dog a woman is using some of my own best moves on me—and they're working! I feel like a dolphin in a tuna net. This one is a keeper.

When the bartender returned with his tequila, Brian leaned in. "See that Latina in the booth over there?"

"She's hard to miss."

"Is she with anyone?"

"Haven't seen anyone man enough yet."

No doubt. That's a whole lot of woman.

"Better get me one of whatever she's drinking." He winked conspiratorially. "I'm going in."

The bartender chuckled. "You're drinking it." "She's drinking tequila neat?"

The Brit behind the bar nodded and poured Brian another Tapatio 110 to match his.

Gorgeous, uses my moves, and drinks my booze. Somebody find me a jeweler!

Brian pocketed his coin and inhaled deeply between his teeth.

I used to dream about the perfect woman but never believed she existed. It's as though the angels hand-picked and delivered her right to my doorstep with a big red bow.

He paid the bartender and left a hefty tip. Tipping well early in the evening was a valuable lesson his mother had taught him. She'd always said women would be impressed with a man who didn't have to wait long for good service, and she was never wrong. Brian had every intention of impressing this woman from the get go – as well as taking her home to meet his mother.

~~~

Jennifer watched as he walked toward her with an extra drink in his hands. His brown eyes sparkled and the slight crow's feet at the edges when he smiled seemed to point to his eyes and say, "You know you want this."

Probably an egomaniac.

He locked his gaze with hers and never once glanced away. Like a cobra moving in for the kill.

I've met too many alpha males to fall that easily. You'll need more than swagger with me.

She let him come over.

Let's see if you've got any substance or you're just a boy out to play.

~~~

Brian couldn't pull his eyes away. They'd been sitting at her table in the lounge, talking for an hour, and he was still mesmerized. He'd asked about her work and she had been animatedly telling him about her current project.

Educated, intelligent, motivated, beautiful. You own me.

Her scent was a delicate mixture of jasmine blossoms and the sea.

Memories of trips to the coast of Aqaba swirled in his mind with those sweet blossoms in bloom on the way to the beach and the sweet, salty scent of the ocean on the wind. Careless moments from his childhood bubbled in his veins, and contentment washed over him. He wanted to swim in her scent.

Her hair rolled down over her shoulders in a gentle tumble of waves. She either spent a great deal of time in the sun or at the hairdresser. By the look of her bronze skin, it was the former. A single lock of her hair dropped down over her left eye and beckoned him as she spoke.

Brian reached over and gently led the stray lock, so soft and smooth, to a spot behind her ear. As he touched her ear, a pink flush rose in her cheeks.

So it's not just me. She feels something here too.

"History tells us the Romans were a land-based people but this ship was loaded down with treasure, much like that coin you have there."

Brian hadn't realized until now he'd been absently rubbing the coin. He always picked up something from the ocean during every mission he'd ever done. This one was during an operation in Algeria, when his team had put the squeeze on Carlos at his estate on the coast. It was the mission where they'd lost Dana.

"Finding this ship could have a serious impact on Roman History as we know it." She motioned toward the coin. "May I see that?"

"Of course." Brian wasn't about to say no to her when the subject was clearly one she was passionate about. She loved what she did and what she did was work in the water. He enjoyed listening to her talk about her work. Her eyes sparkled under long, thick lashes and her face glowed. He watched her examine the coin like a kid at Christmas.

"Do you realize what you have here?"

Brian played dumb. He knew this one coin was worth thousands of dollars but he could never share the circumstances around his finding it. "Yeah, a really great gold coin that fits perfectly in the palm of my hand."

She held the coin up to examine it in the light. "Where did you get this? Did somebody sell it to you?" She handed it back to him.

Brian took the coin and considered it. He knew exactly where he'd found this coin. "No." Memories of his teammate, Dana, flooded his mind. She'd gone off the reservation and decided to tell their mark,

Carlos, that she was with the CIA. The dirtbag let her believe they'd have a life together but once his chopper was in the air, he dropped her out, into the sea below. In order for the team to bring her body home, Brian had to suit up and retrieve her from the sea. Every bone in her body had been crushed by the impact of hitting the water from that height. She had been a flimsy bag of broken bones. He carried the coin as a constant reminder of how tenuous and precious life was in the spy business.

"Brian?" Jennifer laid her hand gently over his. "Are you alright?"

He smiled at the stunning Latina across the table from him. "I picked it up when I was diving off the coast of Algiers."

Her eyes opened wide as she perked up and leaned further forward toward him. "When was that?"

Memories of the firefight with Carlos' bodyguards flashed through his mind. He could smell the sea air and gunpowder like he was there again. "A few years ago."

"What were you doing there? Algeria isn't exactly a tourist destination."

He smiled at her chutzpah. "Work."

Her face flushed pink and she covered it with her hands. "Oh my God." She mumbled. "I'm so sorry." When she moved her hands and looked up at him, she seemed truly embarrassed. "I can't believe I've been talking about myself all this time!"

He laughed as he reached across the table and held her hands. "Don't apologize! You clearly love what you do and I'm fascinated."

By your work and by you.

"You're very kind. I'm not really an egomaniac." She rolled her eyes. "What do you do, Brian?"

Ah, that awkward moment when she asks about my job.

Brian looked around, leaned forward, and motioned with his hand for her to come closer.

She leaned in and he could smell the jasmine again. He took a deep whiff before whispering. "I paint yachts."

She seemed surprised and arched her perfectly groomed brow. "Really?"

This is not some bimbo cruising the Med.

He smiled and sat back in his chair. "Naw. I leave that to the pros. I can't actually tell you what I do. It's too dangerous for you to know."

By the look on her face, he could tell her bullshit meter was banging the code red. For some reason women never believe the truth.

~~~

Being the daughter of a CIA Director, Jennifer had heard that lame-ass line more times than she cared to admit, and it sounded cheesier every time. For some reason, men loved to throw that "secret agent" bullshit around, but having a real spy as a father made drawing the line all the more tedious.

Silly me, I thought you were more than that.

"Oh, please? If I had a dollar for every time I heard that James Bond crap, I'd be a millionaire. If all this was just to play some game then thanks for the drinks." She grabbed her purse and stood.

Brian jumped up from his seat. "Wait!" He touched her arms but didn't grab. "I'm sorry. That sounded really douchey and, truth be told, I used to be that guy."

Okay, none of the James Bond wannabes had ever done this before.

Jennifer wondered what the hell this guy's game was or if he was on the level. "Used to?"

Not many guys would admit to having been a douche.

"Boys grow up." His eyes softened and he seemed sincere. "Sometimes in the blink of an eye."

I can't seem to figure this guy out.

"Look, the truth is I really can't talk about my work. It's not a line and I don't want to play games with you. There are a thousand other things we could talk about. Please stay and have dinner with me?"

He seemed sincere and the chemistry seemed real between them.

A girl's gotta eat, right?

"Alright," she grinned. "But you have to promise me no more spy games."

He held his right hand up. "Scout's honor. Did I mention I was a Boy Scout?" He held her chair as she sat back down and then motioned to the waitress for menus as he returned to his seat.

The crowded lounge seemed empty to Jennifer as they talked about everything and nothing. By the time she noticed the world around them, the moon was high in the sky.

She glanced at her watch. "It's late. I should be getting back. I have to hire a new diver tomorrow." Jennifer grabbed her bag on the seat beside her.

Brian stood. "Mind if I walk you back? We're going the same way and it might look like I'm following you if we don't walk together." She smiled. "Walking together would be nicer. Thank you."

Chapter 5

Brian walked Jennifer down the dock to her slip, right next to where his team had their yacht. When they arrived, Brian touched her elbow gently.

She smiled. "Dinner and drinks were lovely, Brian, but I really do have a lot of work to do in the morning."

She's not that kind of gal. That's refreshing.

"I understand." He lowered his voice slightly in case anyone was listening. "Look, Jennifer, given the incident with Gary earlier today and the fact that it's late and you're alone, I'd really like you to let me check your boat to be sure you don't meet with any more unpleasant surprises. I don't know Gary, or what he's capable of, but if first impressions count for anything, he really doesn't seem like a stand-up guy. I promise I'll go when I know you're safe inside and the Garys of the world – and I are locked out. Would you mind?"

Jennifer's eyes opened wide and she seemed surprised. "That may be one of the sweetest things a man has ever offered to do for me." She pulled a key from her purse and handed it to Brian. "I locked it when I left."

Brian took the key, stepped onto the yacht's deck, and turned to face Jennifer. "Stay there. If the boogeyman shows up, just shout. Jason's cabin is just there and he'll use any excuse to kill a bad man." He turned and strode across the deck toward the glass sliding door that led from the deck to the main salon. He tried the door.

Still locked. I wonder if Gary has a key?

Brian made a quick search of the boat, checking in all the standard Boogeyman spots like inside closets and under beds. He looked around at the posh accommodations. This was no run-of-the-mill marine archaeologist.

She keeps a tight ship, everything seems to be perfectly in place.

After checking both levels of the yacht, as well as the engine room, he climbed the stairs to the main salon and emerged to see Jennifer waiting there with a smile.

"All clear?"

"All clear." He grinned.

"Since you were willing to do all that for me, the least I can do is offer you a drink before sending you on your way."

Chivalry wins!

"I'd love one. Do you have any tequila?" Brian followed her to the bar at the end of the main salon.

"I have several, but I won't waste the good stuff on you if you're going to shoot it and run." She turned away from Brian and opened a cupboard over the bar.

Damn, she's got spunk. But did she just ask me to stay? Lordy, look at that woman! That is an ass I'd die for.

Brian smiled. He was usually much better at reading signals but this woman had him wondering which way was up. "One drink, thoughtfully consumed, and then I'll let you get your sleep."

He touched her shoulders and trailed his fingertips down her ribs to her waist. When she didn't protest, he slipped his hands around her waist. He closed his eyes as he nuzzled her thick, jasmine-scented hair, pushing through the soft waves with his lips so he could reach her elegant, bronze neck.

"Mmm—." She tilted her head away slightly as he kissed her neck.

She tasted as sweet as sugared dates "Ah...amor mio."

My love? What?

Brian opened his eyes and sucked in a breath as he considered the sudden and inappropriate declaration of love.

She turned around to face him and shook her head. "Amor Mio Tequila. Not you, egomaniac."

Holy shit. I am an ass.

Brian grinned and recovered. "Of course. Do you have the Reposado?"

She reached for an ornate ceramic and glass bottle in the cupboard and set it on the bar. "Por supuesto."

Of course.

Brian looked into the open liquor cabinet for the first time and heard the faint singing of angels. He let out a low sigh as he noted the contents. This was no average woman. She had the usual suspects on the bar, Bacardi, Stoli, Gordons, Johnny Walker Blue, but the large cupboard above the bar was a veritable treasure trove of tequilas. A giddiness rose in him like champagne bubbles, as if he were eight years old again, and this was Christmas. He struggled to maintain his composure. The only other woman he knew with a liquor cabinet like that was his own mother, and this was definitely not a "think about mom" moment. He chose the nonchalant approach. "So you like tequila?"

"I'm an aficionado of sorts."

He turned toward her and grinned. "Impressive collection." He reached for the next cupboard door. "Is there more?"

She waved her left hand dismissively. "Please, feel free."

Brian opened the door and hadn't been so overwhelmed with delight since he hitched a ride on a wild dolphin at the age of ten. This woman was beautiful, intelligent, made her life in the water, and knew good tequila.

Thank you, God.

He pointed to a particularly rare bottle. "You don't see this every day."

She smiled. "No, you don't." She poured two snifters of the Amor Mio and replaced the cork. "A friend of mine received it as a gift. This is probably telling about me as a person, but he hated tequila for the typically bad Jose Cuervo tequila experience in college and had no desire to drink it, so I suggested a trade."

"Really? What did you offer, your firstborn?" He eyed her slyly.

She pushed his chest playfully. "Not even close!" She handed Brian his glass. "I gave him a bottle of Johnny Walker."

Touch me again, please?

"Black, Red or Blue?" Brian asked.

A grin spread across her face. "Black."

"You wicked minx!" Brian let out a deep laugh. "You made a profit of at least two grand on that trade!"

She's diabolical and I love it!

Her eyelashes fluttered as she chuckled. "I know!"

Beautiful, smart, and savvy.

Brian couldn't decide what turned him on most: her savvy trade, her delightful laugh, or the fact she didn't show the slightest bit of shame when telling the story. "Well done." He swirled then sniffed the amber liquid inside his glass, still smiling from her story. "So you're more of a collector?"

She sat and motioned for him to sit on the cream-colored, leather sofa beside her. "There are a few brands I follow and I'm always looking for my next conquest, so to speak. You?"

Brian sat sideways so he could face her. Looking into her eyes was like watching the sea, always deep and ever changing. He avoided what might have been a loaded question even though he doubted it was. She carried herself with too much swagger for game-playing. This woman was different. It might kill him, but this one was worth taking slowly. "My family is in tequila. I've been around it most of my life."

"Really? Are they distillers?" She drank a bit of her tequila, paused to savor it, then swallowed.

"No. My mother owns Djinn Tequila." Brian took another drink of the amber spirit in his glass.

Yeah, great. Talk about your mom, dumbass. That'll impress the lady.

Her face lit up. "I've heard of that one! The real magic is in the bottle?"

He nodded and smiled, a little thrill tickled inside him at her knowing the brand's tagline, and took another sip of his drink.

Thank you for not making any mom jokes.

"The blanco is like liquid starlight and worth every penny." She touched his shoulder as she spoke. "I'm curious." Jennifer turned slightly to face him squarely. "The marketing hook is great, but why the name Djinn?"

"It's an homage to my father. He was Arab."

"Didn't you say your name was "Allen"?"

Family history on the first date. There's got to be a rule against that somewhere.

"Al Ahan, actually. My grandparents Americanized it when they emigrated to the United States. It was the 1960's and the world wasn't as inclusive as it is today."

Not that it's inclusive when it comes to Arabs now.

"My grandfather was an archaeologist and went to the United States to teach. Dad was more a man of action than an academic, and stories of genies, the Djinn, fascinated him. When he went missing in action in Viet

Nam, Mom knew he wouldn't be back, so she did what she does to cope, she got busy."

"She started her own tequila brand? Jeez, most women would have taken up ceramics or something. That's a lot of work!"

Wow, she gets it – and didn't freak out about the Arab thing.

He nodded. "Yes, it is. She took us back and forth to Jalisco for years."

~~~

"That was pretty ballsy for a single mother back then. Very impressive," Jennifer agreed.

So that's it. He's the son of a wealthy high-end tequila owner, living it up on his mother's dime.

All evidence said this guy should be a real jerk, but she really wasn't getting that vibe, no matter how hard she looked for it.

"Let's not spend the evening talking about my mother. She'll be happy to talk your ear off when she meets you. Besides, I find you much more fascinating. So what do you do, besides shoot incredibly stupid men with flare guns?"

When she meets me? He's planning on introducing me to his mother? Ug, that public flare gun incident.

She tilted her head, and a lock of hair bounced over her eye. "Not my finest hour, I'll admit, but I didn't appreciate how his little stunt set my schedule back a few days."

Brian leaned in. "Tell me more about this project of yours."

His voice resonated deep within her core, behind her ribs and in her heart.

If he doesn't kiss me soon, I'll have to kiss him.

"I wish I could bore you with that for a few more hours but," she glanced at her watch. "I have to interview new divers and make arrangements for my interns tomorrow. This has been very nice, but I have an early morning with lots to do."

Brian drank the last sip of his tequila and set the glass on the table beside him. "I'll take you to lunch tomorrow and you can tell me all about it."

Assuming the sale? Interesting tactic.

"Thanks, but I don't think so. I'm already behind schedule."

He stood and held his hand out to help her up. "I won't take no for an answer. You'll have to eat eventually. Call me when you're ready. I'm right next door." He pulled a small leather case from his pocket, removed a card, and handed it to her. "I'm sure we could find more to talk about than tequila."

She read the card. "Brian Allen, Maritime Archaeologist."

What are the odds?

She laughed. "All right." She nodded. "Tomorrow, but if I see your boat off the coast of Algiers, I'll assume you're a pirate and, don't forget, I'm pretty handy with a flare gun."

He took her hand and looked into her eyes. "You're really hot with a flare gun." He lifted her chin and kissed her softly on the lips. "If you don't call me by two, I'm coming to get you."

Yes, please?

Chapter 6

Jennifer's daily phone call with her father had turned to the same old topic she didn't care to discuss but he just wouldn't let go. Her mind wandered to Brian's kiss and she felt her cheeks warm.

Her father's voice on the line soon jerked her back to reality. "Mija, stop dreaming about lost treasure and come back to the company."

Kidnappers and terrorists hiding behind their version of "the greater good". It only takes a minute for them to turn on their own.

It always came back to working for the Central Intelligence Agency, working for him. Jennifer stood and paced the floor of the main salon.

"No, Papa. You know I can't."

"Mija, there's no shame in what happened to you. He's the one who was wrong. He lost his career over it. It was years ago and he's not an issue any more."

Jennifer stiffened. "I couldn't work with people like that, Papa. He had no sense of right and wrong. There's no moral compass in the company."

If there were, that agent who kidnapped me would have lost more than his career.

"They aren't all like that, Mija. I work with real heroes every day. Most of them are good people who want to serve their country and keep their loved ones safe."

But they don't mind putting innocents in harm's way, do they? I was innocent.

She shook her head. "Until you show me one, I won't believe you." He sighed. "Just give me the chance."

You have got to be kidding me!

"Of course, Papa! I'll let you know the next time I'll be in Washington and you can call a "bring your daughter to work day" just for me."

"Mija, you know we don't do that here."

Jennifer glared up at the ceiling, wishing she could make him understand she had no interest in becoming an agent for the CIA. "I'm kidding! Papa, I have a good life. I live on a yacht, por Dios!" She wrapped her hands in a death grip around the phone and shook it, then took a breath to compose herself and continued pacing. "Besides, you know Mama would hate it. Why would you ask me to do that? It isn't fair."

Mama worries enough and my biggest occupational hazard right now is sunburn. Imagine how she'd react if I joined the CIA?

This conversation was serving no end but to make the muscles in her neck tense. She rubbed the back of her neck with her free hand.

With every phone call, her father tried to recruit her into the company, and every time she said "no". It had become a point of contention for them, and a pain in the neck, literally and figuratively, for her. "Papa, you were gone your entire career. You're still never home for dinner with her. Birthdays, anniversaries, holidays…you were always a no-show. I realize now I could never live like that, and I won't put Mama through it."

"If you're so concerned about your mama, then why don't you just settle down with a doctor somewhere and give her some grandchildren to dote on?"

I'll have children when I find a man worthy of my eggs. Until then, I will not discuss this with him.

"Why do you insist on doing this dangerous work for pennies? You find millions of dollars' worth of sunken treasure, hand it over to the Smithsonian for nothing, write a report that nobody reads, and you receive no recognition at all."

My father would be happier if I were a pirate. Gah!

"I get plenty of recognition. You just don't read the right periodicals to notice. Besides, you're one to talk about dangerous work for no pay or recognition!"

Damned hypocrite!

"I learned from the best, Papa."

Time for a subject change. Time to piss him off for a change.

"How's that federal budget crisis working for you?"

"You know it isn't an issue anymore, and mine is a career with retirement and health benefits."

She closed her eyes tight, wishing this conversation would go away. "I do it because I'm good at it. I'm at the top of my field, investors are knocking down my door to get on board, and I love what I do."

I need to get off the phone before I lose my temper. I'd tell him my battery is dying but he knows when I'm lying.

"Why do you seem to think my only choices are to do what you want or what Mama wants? Why can't it ever be what I want?"

"Ahh…" He sighed. "There's no talking to you. There's too much of your uncle in you. He filled your head with all that "do what you love" nonsense."

He always has to blame someone else, as though I'm incapable of independent thought.

She took a deep breath to collect herself and calm the frustrations bubbling inside. "No, Papa. It's because you can't control it. Face it. You can't, Mama can't, and that's what sticks in your gut. I'm doing something you have absolutely no control over. You with the company and mama with her social circles, you're both accustomed to having all your people play by your rules, but I chose not to be in either game."

In for a penny, in for a pound. Might as well let him have it.

"I'm not one of your pawns, and I won't be, so get off my back and just let me do what makes me happy."

"You have expertise. You have intelligence. You've had more training than most." His tone softened. "We need more like you in the company. I could assign you anywhere in the world." He was trying to negotiate now. She knew the drill. "You'll have plenty of spare time for your treasure hunts. I could even set you up as a sleeper."

A sleeper agent in the CIA is still an agent.

Her shoulders drooped and she rubbed her forehead. It always had to be on his terms. She glanced out the window and saw Brian waving from his boat. She waved back and her mood lifted.

Brian walked to the dock between their boats and motioned for her to come out.

"I can't discuss this with you anymore." She returned Brian's wave. "I'm late for a lunch meeting now. Goodbye, Papa." She ended the call, slipped the phone in her Coach bag, and ran a brush through her hair before walking out on deck.

You'll need more than steady money and cushy assignments to get me to go to work for the CIA, Papa.

Brian smiled wide as she walked outside. "Hungry yet?" She grinned as she looked him over. "Starving."

~~~

Brian sat back to let the waitress take their empty dishes. "Please tell the chef the roasted Branzino was excellent."

"I will, sir." She nodded and took the dishes back to the kitchen.

Brian focused his attention back on Jennifer. Even small talk with this woman fascinated him. He hung on her every word, laughed at her jokes and wondered how much more he could discover about her before she sailed out of his life.

I wonder if I can keep her here for dinner too – or longer?

As though she'd heard his thoughts, she said, "I've really enjoyed this, but I have to go." She grabbed her bag. "If I'm going to make my timetable and leave in three days, I have to get my crew ready. I have interviews with a few divers this afternoon."

Disappointment washed over Brian but she was still speaking his language. "A diver?" He stood to pull out her chair.

"Yes, I have to replace Gary."

An idea flashed into Brian's mind and he clung to it, grinning from ear to ear. "Oh, the naked guy with the hot girlfriend?"

She laughed. "That's him."

"You know, if you need another naked diver, I'd be happy to help out."

She stood and took a step from the table. "Brian, this is serious."

Brian arched an eyebrow and scowled. "Oh, I take nakedness very seriously."

She touched his cheek with her palm. "You're cute, and sweet, but I would only take you on as crew as my very last resort."

Well, then we'll just have to see to that, won't we?

"You never know when you may need a last resort, complete with naked diver. The offer stands." He offered his hand and she took it and smiled as they walked out of the restaurant and down to the dock. When they arrived at her boat, she tried to let go of Brian's hand, but he held firm. He wasn't about to let her go without plans to see her again. She was leaving in a few days and he didn't want to miss a minute with her. "How about dinner later? I know a great Mexican place."

She laughed. "Mexican in Morocco?"

"Si! Es muy bueno!"

She clasped his hand in both of hers and stepped close enough he could feel her breath as she whispered. "But we just had lunch." She kissed him on the cheek. "Thank you."

Brian let go of her hands and pulled her closer. "It's never too early to plan for your next meal." He kissed her softly and thrilled when she wound her arms around his neck and kissed him back hard.

Or the rest of your life.

Chapter 7

Brian tried to appear busy with his laptop at the table on deck while he quietly watched Jennifer's boat in the next slip. She'd come up every half hour or so and walk around her deck before going back inside.

I feel like a damned stalker. I spy on people for a living but this is the first time its felt weird.

Jason had been quietly sitting on deck, reading his latest copy of Guns & Ammo, when he pulled a pack of cigarettes from the cargo pocket of his trousers. He eyed Brian as he took a cigarette from the pack and lit it. "Dude. Are you waiting for a flare to go up, or what?"

Brian continued to watch the boat in the next slip. She'd been inside for a while now. "I had lunch with her today."

"You what?" Jason sounded incredulous.

"Yeah." Brian sighed as he stood, stretched and then flopped onto a chaise near Jason.

Jason glared at him. "Why aren't you over there now?"

I can't tell him she makes me weak in the knees.

Brian shrugged. "She wouldn't agree to dinner."

Jason jerked upright from his reclining position. "She what?! Oh, bro." He tossed his magazine onto a nearby cocktail table.

Here it comes. The guy who never gets laid is going to give me hell for not being a playboy for once.

Brian nodded. "She's a tough one."

"Bri, we need to talk. We've been living and working together for the agency for a while now."

Years.

"Yeah, we have."

"I can honestly say that in all the time we've been working together, I have never seen you meet a woman who could stay on your mind longer than it took you to shower and dress. Considering her place is just across the plank, I'm a bit confused." Jason took a thoughtful drag on his cigarette and waited for a response.

So am I, brother. Might as well tell him.

He took a deep breath and exhaled before answering. "This woman is different, Jase."

"Aww, shit." Jason looked genuinely surprised as his hazel eyes opened wide. "You fell in love, didn't you?" Jason slapped his thigh and laughed a deep, hearty belly laugh.

Brian nodded. Ego told him to deny it, but the sad truth of the matter was that he had fallen head over heels in love with this woman and he hadn't even slept with her yet. "This is it. This is the woman I want to spend the rest of my life with."

Jason slumped in his chair and shook his head. "You fell hard. Damn."

Brian looked up as a man walked up to Jennifer's boat. "Who's that guy?"

Jason glanced over. "Looks like a diver type to me. Why?"

Looks like he's probably a good diver too. He walks with the swagger of a SEAL and I should know.

"Oh, no you don't." he mumbled. Brian grinned and stood. "Hey champ, you here for the diver job?"

The guy turned toward Brian and nodded. "Yeah, is this the right place?"

Not for you, mister.

"Well, it would have been if you'd gotten here a couple hours ago. You're looking at the new diver. Sorry, man."

Or at least I will be her new diver.

The guy sighed. "Well shit. That was a waste of time. Thanks."

No, thank you for getting away from my girl.

Brian turned toward Jason. "Come on, Jase! Let's go for a walk."

And find that other diver she's got coming by for an interview.

Jason jumped up. "Is there a beer at the end of it?"

"Only if you're very bad." Brian said over his shoulder as he walked briskly onto the dock and headed for the parking lot.

"That's easy enough." Jason chuckled and followed closely behind.

Brian spotted another guy walking down the dock toward them.

Doesn't look yacht club but definitely a working schlub. He must be the other diver.

"Hey, you here for the diver job?"

The man stopped. "Yes, are you the man hiring?"

"I was. I'm sorry to waste your time. I just hired a couple guys. But thanks for coming." Brian smiled his most charming smile. "Leave me your card and I'll call you if we need another." Brian took the man's card and sent him on his way.

That's right, just walk away, pal.

"What are you up to, Bri?"

Brian looked around and figured they'd gone far enough. "Here is good. We're out of earshot and we can see them coming. Smoke 'em if you got 'em."

Jason smirked. "Okay, I see what's up. I'll play your silly game."

I can always count on Jason as a wingman.

Another man walked up to them several minutes later and spoke to Jason. "Excuse me, could you tell me where slip number 30 is?"

Turn him around, bro. He looks like a sleeze.

"Uh, sure. Wait, you aren't signing on as her new diver are you?" Jason snuffed out his cigarette.

"I'm hoping to. It looks like a pretty sweet job. I checked her out on Facebook and she looks hot."

Say one more comment like that and nobody will find your body.

Jason used his most serious tone. "Well, it would be sweet if she weren't batshit crazy. You will never believe what she did to her last diver. Lured him into her cabin, threw all his gear off the boat and into the drink, then she pointed the flare gun at him and kicked him off the boat in nothing but his birthday suit."

The diver gaped. "You're kidding!"

"Nope." Jason shook his head. "That's one crazy bitch."

"Forget that. I can get a diving job somewhere else."

Yes, you can. No off you go.

When the man walked away, Jason grinned at Brian. "Just following your lead, dude. That was fun, but why are we doing this? I thought you liked her."

"We're doing this, Jason, because she said the only way she would sign me on as crew is as a last resort. I have every intention of making her believe that there are no other divers in this world."

Jason grinned. "That's some diabolical shit."

"I know. But it's for a good cause."

Jason nodded. "I can live with that. So this is your idea of a side job, then? Just a little diving gig in the Med?"

Brian grinned and winked. "It could work. Can you keep watch while I go see about a job?"

"Yeah, you got it, dude."

~~~

Brian knocked on the hull. "Permission to come aboard?" Jennifer came out onto the deck and smiled. "Hi there!"

"The sun is going down. Feel like some dinner?"

"Sure. I'm not getting anything done here. Let me get my bag." She went back inside for a moment, came out and locked the door behind her.

Brian reached out with his right hand to help her step onto the dock. "Did you get your diver today?"

"Can you believe I had three guys coming by for interviews and none of them showed up?"

You don't say?

"That's crazy! Did you find them on Craigslist or Sleazy Sailors dot com?"

"No. That's what's really weird about it. They all came highly recommended."

Brian shook his head. "Maybe they just weren't meant to be."

And I am.

Jason greeted them both with a smile as they stepped off the dock and into the parking lot area. "Hey, Brian." He smiled at Jennifer. "Hello, lady. I know you. Flare gun, right?" He gave her his best Cheshire Cat smile. "You two off to dinner?"

Brian suppressed a smile. "Jennifer, this is Jason. We work together."

Jennifer reached her hand out to shake Jason's. "Are you a diver too?"

Jason shook his head as he shook her hand. "I do wet work of a sort, but prefer to keep my head above water."

Jesus, Jason. Why don't you just tell her we're government assassins, you dumbass.

Jennifer didn't seem to get the reference. "Would you like to join us, Jason?" She looked up at Brian. "Mexican food, right?"

Don't you dare.

"Yeah, Jason can't do Mexican food." Brian took Jennifer's hand and hoped Jason would take the hint. "He's deathly allergic to cilantro." He winked at Jason. Jason made a show of checking his pockets and laughed. "Haven't got my epi pen. Thanks anyway. You kids have a good time. It was very nice meeting you, flare gun." He walked back toward the slip where American Swift's yacht was, chuckling as he went.

"He's a funny one," Jennifer remarked.

"That he is." Brian nodded. "But he's a good man to have on your side."

"I wonder if he realizes that the term "wet work" is spy talk for assassinations?"

Jesus, she caught it!

Brian played dumb. "Is it really? How do you know that?"

Jennifer paused for an uncomfortable moment. "Oh, I don't know. Watching movies, I guess."

~~~

They'd had cocktails, appetizers, salads, a main course, and bright conversation. Brian decided it was time to make his move. "So, are you ready to sign me on yet?"

"Not yet. I still have one that's going to call me about an interview tomorrow."

Shit.

"I could call you if you gave me your number."

"But why bother when you're right next door?"

"I won't always be. Don't you have a business card?"

She laughed, wiped the corners of her lips with a napkin and stood. "Excuse me. Ladies room. I'll be right back."

Brian watched her walk to the ladies room and then snatched her phone from where she'd left it on the table. "Obviously you don't realize who you're dealing with, sweetheart." He dialed his own phone, waited a moment for the call to register, and then hung up, placing her phone just as she had left it. He then picked up his own phone and quickly added her number to his contacts, typing in the words "Mrs. Brian Allen".

She'll come around.

A wave of familiar, yet overwhelming, perfume wafted over him as a hand massaged his shoulder. "Hello, handsome." He looked up as blonde hair tumbled over his shoulder and someone tried to examine his phone screen. He clicked the screen off immediately.

"Finally getting around to calling me?"

"Hello, Pamela." He'd passed an unremarkable evening with her several weeks ago. She didn't warrant a follow up, so he never did call her. Other than the way she looked in a dress she really had no qualities that made him think that she might be long term material. "I thought you were off to Cannes?"

I wish you were in Cannes because this could be awkward.

She perched in Jennifer's seat and purred. "Not yet." She leaned across the table, pressing her thirty-eight double Ds even closer together. "Let's go to my place."

"As appealing as that is, I'm here with someone. It's a business meeting. You understand?" He stood to try to usher her out but she clearly had no intention of leaving.

"Oh, I can wait." She murmured.

No, no, no. You need to go. You are not the kind of woman other women want to feel they're competing with.

Brian grew more nervous with every passing moment. Pamela was a knockout but they had agreed their night together was just some fun between friends. While it was fun, Brian was completely off the market. He had no intention of disrespecting Jennifer by having Pamela's boobs here when Jennifer got back. "Sorry. You've got to go, darlin'. It was fun but we both know that's all it was."

Jennifer chose that moment to walk out of the ladies room and the cloud that fell over her face was unmistakable.

I'd rather get shot with a flare gun than ever see that look on her face again.

Jennifer walked straight to the table, never acknowledged Pamela or Brian, picked up her phone and purse, and walked out.

Shit!

Pamela smiled and either played dumb or really was. Brian knew it was a toss-up. "Who was that?"

Brian pulled out his wallet and left enough cash on the table to cover dinner and a hefty tip for the waiter. "That, my silly little bit, is the woman I'm going to marry." He jogged out of the restaurant and looked up and down the street for Jennifer. She was nowhere to be seen and he suddenly felt it like a stone in his gut.

Maybe she caught a taxi back?

Brian jogged back toward the dock and finally caught up with Jennifer after two blocks.

Damn, did she run in those heels?

"Jennifer! Jennifer, wait."

She waved him off without even turning around or breaking pace.

He closed the gap and caught up with her. "Jennifer, that wasn't what you think."

She glared at him. "Brian, I'm not into drama. I don't care that you're seeing other women. I just don't think dinner with me is a good time to do it."

Fair enough.

Pamela had that effect on other women. Brian tried to explain.

"No, it wasn't like that."

She kept walking at a fast clip and didn't turn to face him. "That's okay. It's all right, Brian. Honestly, I really don't care."

But I do!

Brian lurched ahead and turned to face her, looking into her eyes. "Why don't you?"

She stopped and shrugged, but despite her efforts, Brian could see she was pissed. Her jaw was clenched and her pupils were slightly dilated. "It's really none of my business. We aren't exclusive. We aren't even dating. I have no business telling you what you can and cannot do, just like you don't have any business telling me what I can and can't do." She stepped around him and continued toward the dock.

Exasperated, Brian shouted at her back. "But I want you to tell me what to do!"

Holy hell, that sounded stupid!

She stopped short, paused, and finally turned around. "You what?"

Tell her you care. Tell her she's important. Tell her you've fallen head over heels for her. No, don't tell her that yet.

"Well I don't want you to tell me what to do, but I would like you to care what I do." He took long strides to catch up with her.

She shook her head and gaped at him. She held her right hand up. "Look, you're handsome and interesting and I really like you, but I don't play games like that and I neither expect nor tolerate being played. Thank you for dinner. Goodnight." She turned on her heel and walked to her boat.

Way to go, jackass. If she gets away, you'll never forgive yourself.

He jumped over her boat's rail and blocked her door before she could unlock it. He grabbed her by the shoulders and pulled her to him, pleading with his eyes and praying to God he'd stop sounding like an idiot. "Look Jennifer, no other woman matters. I don't know who you are but I know I'm ready to spend the rest of my life finding out."

"What?! What are you saying to me?"

"I'm trying to say that I'm crazy about you and I--. I want us to be together."

She smiled as one would to a small child or a lost puppy and spoke softly. "We're together until we're not together. Like here, now, we're together." She shoved him out of the way and unlocked her door. "In just a moment," her tone was hard and her voice loud, "I'm going to board my boat and you aren't. Then we won't be together."

"Damnit, woman!"

She stepped inside and slammed the sliding glass door closed.

Time for the Hail Mary, Brian.

"I'm in love with you!" He shouted through the glass.

She opened the door but stayed on her side of it. "That's the most ridiculous thing I've ever heard! We are, literally, two ships passing." She pointed to his boat and then back to hers. "I have work to do on a timetable and I don't plan to give that up for a romp in the sack with some jet-setting playboy who's used to getting his way with every woman he meets."

Brian placed his hands on either side of the door opening and looked into her beautiful brown eyes. "Jennifer, I'm not asking you to give anything up. I'm telling you I'll give up mine. Let me come with you?"

And please stop making me beg out here because we're going to draw an audience.

It finally seemed to register. "Oh my God, you're serious?"

"I'm serious as a heart attack. Besides I've always wanted to be a pirate. You need a diver, and I'm the best in the business. Come on, say yes!"

"You're crazy!"

"Crazy in love."

She shook her head. "You'd better go, I have to leave in the morning."

"What?"

Did she just shut me down?

"My crew will be here at seven. We're leaving on the tide. I have an assignment, people to report to. This is not time for a Mediterranean romp. I've got work to do."

What the hell?

Brian shook his head, flabbergasted. He was sure she had been falling for him too. "But--?" Confusion consumed Brian.

Jennifer closed the door again and locked it. "I'll call you," she shouted from inside.

"Jennifer?"

"I'm not blowing you off. I really do have to go tomorrow and there's too much riding on this job. Your timing sucks." She closed the curtain.

Brian picked up the pieces of his never-before-broken heart and walked back to his boat in a daze.

Chapter 8

The whole team was assembled and having drinks on the deck as the lights of Morocco grew smaller. Jay and Sarah had arrived from Moscow that afternoon, and the team was headed out to sea for the privacy to debrief without the risk of being overheard. Sarah and Jay had been in deep cover with the Russian Mafia for nearly a year now.

Every few months, they'd come back to Morocco for a full debrief. While they were in Moscow, the rest of the team, Brian, Jason, Will and Chris, their communications guy, were basically sleeper agents.

Brian poured two glasses of tequila and handed one to Jason as he took his seat at the dining table. They rarely used the formal dining room, but when they did, it was like a family dinner and all topics were fair game.

Jason seemed completely bewildered. "You told her you were in love with her and then she just left the love thing hanging like that? No explanation, just the bum's rush?"

Brian nodded and took a sip of his drink. "Yeah."

"Dafuck? That never happens to you." Jason shook his head like something was loose inside.

"Sorry, mate." Jay frowned.

Brian liked Jay and thought one of their heated games of darts might be in order tonight. Jay Stanstead had made his career in the British Army's Special Air Service (SAS) but was hired as a freelancer to work as Sarah Stevens' bodyguard. As it turned out, he and Sarah got along great and worked together like a well-oiled machine, so he was hired by the CIA to stay on indefinitely. He'd become family in no time at all.

Sarah spoke up. "At the risk of seeming insensitive, it looks to me like the player finally got played." She nudged Brian, seated next to her. "How many women and their panties have fallen for you over the years?"

If I didn't love you like a sister, I'd blow up your car for that, Sarah Stevens.

Brian winced as he put his arm around Sarah's shoulders. "Yeah, I guess I was due. But to lose you and then her? That's just too cruel."

Sarah pursed her lips into a pout. "Oh, Brian."

"Have a care, lad." Jay warned as he removed Brian's arm from Sarah's shoulders and eyed him behind her back. "Those are shark infested waters you're swimming into."

I'd blow up a small nation to have what those two have.

Brian winked. "No hard feelings, man. You and Sarah are great together."

~~~

Jennifer woke with a start. She opened her eyes to pitch blackness and the sound of breaking glass on the upper deck.

This isn't the crew arriving to prep the boat.

Heavy footsteps ran through the main salon and she heard two men talking.

Stay calm. Get the gun.

The hairs on her arms and the back of her neck stood up as cold shot through her body from head to toe. This wasn't just a robbery. She reached for the gun in the drawer of her bedside table.

Memories flashed into her mind of her training at The Farm. One of the CIA trainers had taken her in the middle of the night. The other trainees thought it was part of the training, so no one said anything about it until morning.

The gun is gone! This is impossible. I've kept it there since I purchased the boat.

She searched the whole drawer frantically and the gun wasn't there.

Memories of her kidnapping while in training with the CIA came flooding back like strobe light flashes.

He'd put a bag over her head and stripped her naked, tying her to the wall and torturing her for hours. When exhaustion had finally set in, he'd thrown her against a cold table and held her down. Had the other instructors not tracked him down in time, had they not broken in when they did, he'd have raped her and left her for dead. He said as much in his statement.

Her doorknob rattled as someone tried it and she jerked back to the present.

Shit, shit, shit! It can't be Brian. He wouldn't do that, would he?

A rush of panic washed over her. She knew human trafficking was a very real threat. After all, she had to be insured for kidnap and ransom by virtue of her work. Insurance was no reason not to take every safety precaution available.

Someone banged on her door and she heard a voice say "Check the other cabins, just in case."

Could this be Papa's attempt at intimidation? He's turned spies for years. What's to say he wouldn't try to intimidate his own daughter to get his way?

She rolled to the far side of the bed and felt between the mattress and box spring for the knife she always kept there. When a woman traveled all over the world in a yacht, she had to be prepared, and that meant backing up her backup.

Someone was kicking her door now. It wouldn't be long before it gave way.

Jennifer pulled the Gerber from its hiding place as she slid off the side of the bed, keeping the queen sized comfort top between her and whoever was now attempting to break down the door.

She reached for her cell phone on the nightstand with her free hand just as the cabin door flew open. Startled, she fumbled with the keys to hit redial and finally managed it. He father wanted her in the company, but even he wouldn't endanger her like this.

Would he?

Two men with handguns lurched into her bedroom. One stopped at the door, blocking it, and the other walked toward her purposefully with long strides. She stayed crouched by the bed and held the knife in her right hand while she held the dialing phone in her left, behind her back.

The larger of the two men crossed the room in two steps, squinted at her, and tucked his Heckler & Kock nine millimeter into the back of his waistband.

Other girls learned to identify flowers. Jennifer grew up learning to identify weaponry.

"Gimme that knife before you hurt yourself, girlie." He reached to take it from her.

Try to take it, you son of a bitch.

"Get off my boat." She jumped up and evaded his grasp with a quick twist of her arm and cut his meaty forearm with a neat four-inch slice.

He grinned but looked not at all amused. "Oh, kitten's got claws, huh? He shoved her against the wall and grabbed the knife, throwing it behind him. It stuck in the cabin wall.

Can I reach his gun? The guy at the door doesn't look fast enough and I could use this guy as a shield. I need that gun.

"Look sweetheart," he pressed her against the wall with his left hand against the base of her neck as he licked the cut on his right arm and smiled. "Just come along with us and you'll be fine. Do what we say and we won't have to hurt you."

She tried to reach around him with her free hand but he was too big and her reach wasn't long enough.

"Oh, no. Girls shouldn't play with guns." He spoke low and menacing and his breath stunk of garlic.

She had no idea if she had managed to dial her father or not. He was the only person she ever called, and would know what to do if he couldn't reach her. She just had to stay calm and get as much information as she could just in case the call had gone through and her father was listening.

But what if it was Papa who set all this into motion? He had the resources to put something like this together. But what if he hadn't?

She spoke loudly so her father could hear her. "Who are you? Who do you work for? You there at the door, five foot ten white guy with blond hair and military-style buzz cut, who hired you and your six-foot-four redheaded goon to break into my boat? Did my father send you? That's just precious, Papa. Sending two men to kidnap me from my boat? Seriously?"

The man at the door, the one pointing a Glock at her, tilted his head quizzically like a confused dog. He glanced at his partner. "Why is she describing me?" Then he stared at Jennifer. "What kind of crazy bitch are you?"

Not very quick, are you? These guys can't be CIA.

Jennifer hoped his huge friend would be just as dumb.

"She's not crazy, you dumbass. She's got a phone behind her back."

Come on, Papa!

The brains of the outfit had a steady stream of blood trickling down his arm but pressed himself against her. He sandwiched her between his tall, hard body and the wall. Her hand, still behind her and holding the phone, was crushed between her and the wall, but she continued to hope someone was on the other end of the line.

She squirmed and tried to wriggle free but he was like a concrete wall. "Let me go!" She yelled as loudly as she could. "Help!" She tried to claw at him with her free hand but it was no use.

He grabbed her by the neck and ground his hips against her. It was obvious that kidnappings turned this guy on.

Panic coursed through her as she flashed back to her previous kidnapping.

He's going to rape me.

Cold fear gripped her as she struggled to breathe.

He let his left hand creep down to cup her breast, his meaty bleeding forearm pressed against her shoulder so she couldn't move. He breathed heavily into her ear with rancid breath while she squirmed, unable to wedge herself out from under the hold he had her in. "I don't know or care who your daddy is, sweetheart. I get paid as long as I bring you in alive."

After several breaths she tried to slide out from between him and the wall but he just pressed harder.

"Nothing in my contract says I can't have a little fun with you before I bring you in."

"I promise you it won't be fun." A whisper was all she could manage with his hand wrapped around her neck. "I'll die first."

He reached around her and grabbed the phone, copping a feel of her ass as he did. "Nice." He pressed himself against her as he looked at the phone.

She heard a faraway voice at the other end. "Jennifer, if you can hear me, stay calm. I'll find you."

Brian's voice? But how?

"We're just having a little fun with you, pal." The kidnapper hung up on Brian and then threw the phone behind him.

The statement did little to calm her. Brian's boat had sailed out shortly after she sent him away. He was nowhere near here and, even if he had been, what would he know about fighting off kidnappers? Her heart pounded in her chest as she realized it might take days for her father to get word she'd been kidnapped. Brian was an amateur. What good could a marine archaeologist do against kidnappers? Fear wrapped itself around her chest like a serpent and squeezed hard.

But what if Papa arranged this to make me finally face my demons over being kidnapped while in training?

"Okay, so what's the plan? Kidnap me, make me stew in my own sweat for a couple days? Scare me straight or make me get off on the adrenaline? Is that what the old man has in mind?"

The big man pressing himself against her and towering over her, narrowed his eyes as he glared at her. They were the color of tiger eye stones and they were just as cold. "Sorry, girlie. There is no question and answer part of this show. He reached into her closet and grabbed a pair of shorts and a T- shirt. Now unless you want to push me any further to see what I might do to that tight little ass of yours, you're going to put these on and take a little trip with us." He threw the clothes at her. "Now get dressed."

She picked up the clothes and tried to stall. "That's okay, I take trips all the time. I'm on one right now, and a lot of people are expecting me to be somewhere shortly, so if you'll just be on your way, I can keep my schedule. I'll just write you a check and we can forget all about this."

The force of the back of his hand meeting her jaw threw her into the wall. She crumpled, stunned from the impact of both his hand and the wall.

"I said get dressed." He growled.

She stayed seated on the floor but slipped the shorts on. "I-I'm sure you boys are just doing your jobs, but I can match whatever it is you're getting paid for this and we can just call it a misunderstanding."

Please take a payoff. Please?

She slipped the T-shirt on over her head and the short nightgown she had worn to bed. "If this is my father's doing, please tell him I'm tired. I have work to do in the morning and really don't have time for this nonsense anymore. Just call him and tell him to go fuck himself. Tell him this is the worst job offer in the history of job offers."

The big man, now standing over her, knotted a mass of her hair in his meaty fist and pulled her to her feet. "You want to play? This is not a game. I don't know who your father is, and I don't care."

Oh my God. I think these guys are for real. But if Papa didn't send them, who would?

He slammed his hips against her. He wasn't fooling around. His cold gaze burned into her as he growled, "You're a pretty thing and I just love making Latinas scream, so unless you want me to string you up like a pinata and have my way with you right now, you'd better shut up and do what I say, girlie. Play time is over."

Jennifer swallowed hard but the lump of disgust and anger in her throat wasn't going anywhere.

Not again. No way. Not again.

The big man glared at her. "Okay, let's go. He had the handgun in his left hand and grabbed her hair with his right, pushing her ahead of him at arm's length. "And just in case there's any doubt..." he pulled her hair hard, spinning her around and forcing her to her knees on the floor in front of him. "I'm in charge here."

The pain from every hair on her head being pulled made her vision blur and her eyes water. Uncontrollable tears welled in her eyes as he pulled her head back, making her look up at him.

"Do you understand now?"

She choked on the tears. "Yes."

Chapter 9

Brian paced the deck as Will sat down at the dining table and took a sip of his coffee. "Okay, Brian. What's so important you had to roust me out of bed before sunrise, and why are your bags packed as though you're going somewhere?"

Because I am.

Brian sat in a chair across from him and laced his fingers together on the table in front of him. "I'm taking some leave."

Will raised a brow. "Oh, really? How long?"

"A month. Jennifer needs a diver on a wreck off Algeria. Sarah, Jay and all of you have things here pretty much wrapped up. If something happens and you need backup, you know I can get back fast and cover your six. I'm a sleeper here anyway. Might as well keep busy, right?"

"Hmm." Will looked thoughtful as he took a long drink of his coffee. "It might be good for you." He nodded. "Do it. I'll smooth things over with the Director."

Brian's phone rang. He glanced at the caller identification and smiled before answering. "Hey, Jennifer. I knew you'd need a diver. I'm packing my gear now."

Her voice was muffled but he could just make out what she said so he listened.

Who butt dials at this hour?

Her voice sounded shaky. "Who are you? Who do you work for? You there at the door, five foot ten white guy with blonde hair and military-style buzz cut, who hired you and your six-foot-four redheaded friend to break into my boat? Did my father send you? That's just precious, Papa. Sending goons to kidnap me? Seriously?"

What the hell?

A man's voice sounded distant. "Why is she describing me? What kind of crazy are you?"

Good girl. Give me more information.

A different man's voice was closer to the phone. "She's not crazy, you dumbass. She's got a phone behind her back."

Time to go!

Adrenaline shot through Brian's system with the force of a fire hose.

He put the phone on speaker so Will could hear it and grabbed a pen and paper that were nearby on the table. He wrote down the descriptions Jennifer had mentioned and passed them to Will.

"Have Chris track her boat." He wrote the name of her boat on the paper.

He grabbed his phone and spoke clearly. "Jennifer, if you can hear me, stay calm. I'll find you."

How the hell did she get targeted for kidnapping and why would she think her father was in on it?

Brian ran inside and leapt down the stairs to the team's quarters.

"Jason!" Three paces and he landed at Jason's cabin door, banging on it like police before a raid. "Jase! Get the zodiac. I'm getting guns."

Jason whipped open his cabin door and stood wide-eyed in a pair of tightie-whities. "Somebody say guns? Are we getting the band back together? Do we have a mission?"

You're damned right we do.

"I'll brief you on the way in." Brian punched in the code to open the arms locker the previous owner had custom installed in the hallway between the cabins. The door to the locker sprang open automatically within seconds and he grabbed a couple .40 caliber handguns. "Damsel in distress stuff." He grabbed two clips in each hand and pocketed them.

"Damsel in distress? Yes!" Jason did a fist pump on his way out of his cabin, gripping a pair of shorts and a T-shirt tightly in his hand. "Gratitude sex," he sang as he ran up the stairs to the main deck. Jason never let clothes hold him back from being first on scene when the shit hit the fan.

Brian followed closely behind, grabbing the two bags he'd already had packed and waiting on deck.

Jason tossed his handful of clothes into the Zodiac, jumped in and started the engine.

Will shook his head and pointed a knowing finger at Brian. "Don't call me from a Moroccan jail. You know we're here on non-official cover. Anybody needs killing, you clean it up when you're done."

Brian threw his gear into the Zodiac. "Wilco."

Jason untied the zodiac, the small Kevlar boat they kept ready for getaways and special operations, as Brian jumped in. "Mission brief?"

"Remember Jennifer?"

"Flare gun? Hottest of hotties and your future wife? Brother, do I!" Jason put the boat in gear and pushed the accelerator as far forward as it would go. He pointed it in the direction of the port.

"I think she's being kidnapped." Brian handed Jason a gun.

"No shit?" Jason grinned as he looked at the gun. "SIG Sauer p226. Nothing like a firefight before breakfast. Mag me."

What a maggot. Jason is definitely the best guy to have my six.

Brian nodded, handing Jason two magazines as he attempted to call Jennifer back. The phone just rang and finally went to voice mail.

She's definitely against game playing so this has to be the real thing.

He slipped his phone back into his pocket and watched anxiously as the zodiac sped toward the yachts sleeping in their slips.

How much of a lead do they have on us?

The cool morning air filled Brian's lungs as the speeding Zodiac churned the blue black Mediterranean waters into whispering white froth.

~~~

Jennifer knew no one heard her muffled screams as the men dragged her, hands bound and mouth gagged with her favorite Hermes scarves, from her boat to a small speed boat. If any of the neighbors did hear her, they'd just grown used to the scenes coming from her boat lately and ignored it. Nobody would hear her shouts over the whining of the speed boat motor either. She kicked at them the entire way. If she could kick them overboard, she might be able to maneuver the speedboat to shore for help. The sun had just come up, bleeding red across the sky.

Red sky at morning, sailor take warning.

Jennifer looked carefully at the men on either side of her. This wasn't just her father trying to intimidate her. Even her father wouldn't be so cruel. She continued kicking at them until she no longer had the energy.

Whoever was behind this was paying these men a whole lot of money if they couldn't be bought off. After several minutes at full throttle, they finally pulled up beside an older model yacht, anchored just over the horizon.

I don't recognize that boat. Who is behind this?

The larger man pulled her from the motorboat to the kidnappers' yacht and shoved her up the stairs into a modest main cabin.

She continued to fight the natural response to panic and remembered the training she'd had at the CIA. She counted silently to maintain steady breathing as they ushered her down a narrow stairway and into a tiny cabin below. Once inside, they untied her and removed the gag.

"It took you long enough to get her here."

It can't be him!

She recognized the voice as the man appeared at the cabin doorway. The shock of it hit her like a hard punch to the gut. "Gary?"

"Hello, Jenny." He placed special emphasis on the name "Jenny," and its effect was the same as fingernails on a chalkboard.

Mutherfucker!

"You son of a bitch!" Jennifer dove through her captors in a frenzy and flung herself toward Gary, wrenching free from one man and taking the other with her.

Gary stepped back just enough to stay out of reach.

"And here I thought my father was behind all this! I knew you'd do something sleazy, but never thought you'd have the balls to do something like this." She clawed at him but her fingernails came up centimeters short. "My family won't pay you a dime. My father will have you skinned alive if my mother doesn't beat him to it!"

He stepped back and waved a hand dismissively as the kidnappers grabbed her arms and pulled her back. "Yeah, yeah, whatever."

Whatever? You stupid fool. You're a dead man.

She struggled against their grips on her arms. "You're ruined. You're a dead man!" She spat at him, finally making contact with a wad of spit in his eye.

"Lock her up!" He swiped the spit off his face with the back of his hand.

In what twisted universe does a douchebag like Gary call the shots?

The larger of the two kidnappers threw her against the wall, face first, pinning her and twisting her arm behind her back.

Pain wrenched from her face down to her shoulder. A low growl of anger rose in her throat. She swallowed hard as the vise-like grip of a huge meaty hand crushed her wrist.

Remember your training. You can turn this around. These guys are guns for hire, mercenaries, not highly-trained spies.

Flashbacks from her first kidnapping, when she'd been thrown into walls for hours, overwhelmed her. She stopped struggling, knowing it would only make things worse. Adrenaline continued to course through her veins as she attempted to slow her breathing.

Pain shot through the back of her head just before she blacked out.

Chapter 10

Brian boarded Jennifer's yacht while Jason stayed aboard the Zodiac, scanning the horizon in the pre-dawn light. "Bri, status?" I've got a small motorboat just short of the horizon."

Brian emerged from the salon. "Get a bearing on it. The boat is clear. There was a struggle in her cabin. She's not here."

Knife in the wall, broken closet door, a nightstand drawer on the floor. What the hell went on here?

"Bri, I'd know those legs anywhere. She isn't going willingly either. There are two men with her. We'll never catch up with those guys. They're moving fast, and my guess is they've got a yacht and backup just over the horizon."

A phone rang below deck.

Jason looked up at Brian. "You hear that?"

Brian ran toward the sound. "Yeah, let's hope it keeps ringing so I can find it. Maybe it's the kidnappers." He found the phone on her bedroom floor and knew immediately why she might think her father was in on the kidnapping.

Fuck me!

"Jason, you're not gonna believe this." Brian returned with a phone in his hand. "Three missed calls." He showed the screen to Jason.

Jason glanced at the screen. "From 'Dad'. Well that's a whole lot of nothing."

The one time all he has to do is look at the picture and he chooses to read.

"No, Jase. Look at the picture of 'Dad'."

"Dude looks familiar. Why do I know that face?"

"Director Santiago, Special Activities Division. Ringing any bells yet?"

"Jesus, fuck! You hooked up with the boss' daughter?"

What are the odds?

The phone rang again. "It's him."

Jason nodded. "His daughter just got kidnapped. He's been compromised. Take it."

Brian clicked on the call. "Hello."

This could either go very well or very badly. My money is on badly.

A stern voice on the other end spoke. "Who is this?"

The important thing is to confirm your identity, mister.

"My name is Brian, but I think the more important question here, sir, is who you are."

"Where is my daughter?"

"Is this line secure, sir?"

"All right, you son of a bitch, who are you and what have you done with my daughter?"

Okay, good response from a father but directed at the wrong guy.

"We're wasting time. If you are who I think you are, you'll put in a secure call to Agent Allen through Tango Foxtrot One Two Fife Alpha Sierra. If you aren't, I suggest you call the U.S. Embassy in Tanger, your daughter has been kidnapped."

Ain't nobody got time for that "who's your daddy?" shit.

~~~

Director Florio Santiago hung up his phone and glared up at his secretary as she walked into his office.

"Sir, we've received some disturbing intelligence."

"You don't say?" A quick glance at his desk clock informed him it was ten pm.

He had safeguards in place so that his daughter didn't get kidnapped and he needed to know where she was, if she was safe, and who was going to burn for it.

Abby closed the door behind her and spoke in a hushed tone as she walked closer toward his desk. "The listener you put on your daughter's yacht just called me. Two men broke into her boat and kidnapped her approximately one hour ago. Aerial surveillance confirms this."

"Are you tracking them?" Florio had known it was just a matter of time before his daughter was kidnapped again. If it wasn't her work in some of the most dangerous seas in the world, it would be her connection to him. "Where did they take her?"

Abby placed a map showing the location and a transcript of the event in front of him on his desk. "They transported her via speedboat to a small yacht anchored about a half-mile out to sea. We're tracking it now. It appears to be staying close to the coastline."

"Thank you, Abby. Please make this a priority and keep me updated on where they're going."

"I thought you'd feel that way, sir, so I took the liberty of creating a case number." She pointed to the paperwork on his desk. "You can log in and track it from your computer."

"Good job. Thank you very much, Abby. Standard protocols apply."

That's what I'm supposed to say, but I'm going off the reservation anyway.

She nodded. "Of course, sir."

"And Abby, would you place a call to Agent Allen, Task Force 125, American Swift?"

"You mean to his handler, sir?"

"No, I want to talk to him directly and on a secure line."

She knows that's not standard protocol.

"Immediately, sir." The pencil-thin brunette turned on her toe and left the office quickly and quietly.

She'd be a great field agent if I didn't need her here.

Florio read quickly through the transcript.

She thinks I'd have her kidnapped?

When he'd read all the information, he took a deep breath. What he was about to do wasn't the accepted procedure at all, but this was his daughter, and he wasn't about to take any chances. Jennifer had K&R insurance which meant she was four times more likely to survive a kidnapping than someone who wasn't insured.

But what if they aren't after the money? What if they planned to sell her?

Frustration boiled inside him. This was his daughter! He punched the intercom button and tried not to shout. "Abby, who do I have to fire to get a call with Agent Allen? Put him through on a secure line as soon as you can."

"Yes, sir."

He shuddered as he considered the possible outcomes of this scenario. Standard protocol demanded they wait for a ransom call before sending in a negotiator. Florio knew the first twenty-four hours were crucial, and he wasn't about to wait for the kidnappers to call him before taking action.

I'm the Director of the National Clandestine Service of the United States Central Intelligence Agency. Nobody steals my daughter and lives.

The intercom beeped. "American Swift on line two, sir."

He snatched the phone and held it to his ear. "Line secure?"

"Yes, sir."

"Who am I speaking to?" "Agent Will Adams, sir."

"Adams, I need to speak to Agent Allen A.S.A.P."

"Yes, sir. As his team leader, may I ask what this is in regards to?"

"No, you may not. Put Allen on the damned line!"

Yeah, because the Director calls agents just to fucking chit-chat.

"Just a moment, sir."

~~~

Brian pulled his phone from his pocket and waited. It took less than a minute to ring. Will's voice, overly calm and instantly foreboding, emanated from the speaker. "Brian, you have a phone call from the Director."

Yep, that's Daddy alright.

"I was expecting one."

Will's voice came again, only this time there was a bit of an edge to it. "Is there something you should brief me about?"

Nah, you'll put it together.

Brian shrugged. "Jennifer is Santiago's daughter."

Will's voice was a rough whisper. "The fuck, you say! I'm putting the call through now."

"Agent Allen speaking."

A soft-voiced female spoke. "Director Santiago, Agent Allen is on the line."

"Agent Allen?"

"Yes, sir."

"Where's my daughter and how are you involved?"

"She called me when it happened. Agent Williams and I responded immediately, but she'd already been taken to another boat."

"Yes, I know. We're tracking it now. I need this conversation to be completely off the record. Do you have any moral objections to pulling away from your current assignment to handle this?"

And here I thought I'd have to lie about going AWOL.

"Sir, none at all. Do you have a kidnap and ransom specialist on this? If you ask me, you need to get the professionals in here. There are better people with much more expertise than I in that field. If you need something destroyed, I'm your agent, but I don't negotiate..."

"Shut up, Allen. We're wasting time here." The director was scared, and for good reason.

"Yes, sir."

"I've got our best K&R people on the job. I don't give a rat's ass about protocols. I know what your team did to Federov and I want you to handle this particular case the same way, completely off the books. I want my daughter returned unharmed, and those bastards that took her destroyed. Can you do this?"

Now we're talking!

"Absolutely. Chris has already satellite tagged the speedboat they used and is tracking the boat they took her to." Brian's mind focused on the mission.

Decimate bad guys and save the girl.

"What do we have for resources?"

"There is no we. I can't free your team without days' worth of paperwork and senate sub-committee hearings. I need you to handle this yourself."

Bring back the girl or return in a body bag. Typical Tuesday.

Brian had always worked with teams, SEAL teams, task force teams. This would be a solo gig. His mind was already swimming in the questions he needed to ask, but one thought permeated his entire being.

I can't allow anything to happen to Jennifer.

"I'm walking a tightrope on this one, Agent Allen. I want you to track her, but don't interfere unless negotiations break down or she's in danger."

What? That doesn't make sense.

Brian ran his fingers through his hair. "She has been kidnapped. I'd say that's pretty dangerous already. You just want me to tail her?"

Somebody must have walked into his office. Of course, that's it.

"I want you to be her guardian fucking angel! Do you understand what sort of situation I'm in here Allen? I'm in a very delicate position and certain people could see this as compromising me. If those people start questioning my integrity and my ability to do my job, then we're in a whole world of shit."

"Understood, sir."

"I want you to tail her and report to me regularly. I want to know where they are and that she's safe. If it goes sideways, I want you to pull her out by any means necessary. Do you understand what I'm asking?"

Yeah, rescue your daughter but don't let congress know you're abusing your position because the Secretary of State will get her panties in a twist. Family dysfunction or politics, both suck.

"Yes, sir."

"Can you do it?"

"Yes, sir."

"We don't go tactical until the situation demands it."

As far as Brian was concerned, the situation had already called for it. Unless the Director was a Class-A douchebag, Brian understood what he was really asking. The old man could say what he liked, and as long as he had plausible deniability when the shit went down, his ass would be covered and his cushy job would remain secure.

I hate desk jockeys.

"Yes, sir."

Rest assured, the shit is going down.

Chapter 11

Florio knew this could be the end of his career one way or the other. If his daughter was lost or any harm came to her, he could never live with himself, much less do the job he did every day. If he pulled strings, it would put his integrity and security clearances in question.

Lose his daughter or lose his clearance? There wasn't a choice. In all the years he had worked in the field, a lack of integrity was considered an asset as long as it was used for the benefit of the United States. All that mattered was doing the right thing by whatever means necessary. The right thing to do now was to get his daughter back by whatever means necessary. Even if it meant unleashing American Swift.

~~~

Brian knew time was off the essence. "Leave me the guns and ammunition, Jason. Take the Zodiac back. I'll take her boat."

"Bullshit, I'm coming with you. You need backup for something like this."

"No, Jason. You'll be more help to me back with the team. If it goes sideways, I may need some resources."

"All right, man." Jason untied the yacht from the dock. "I'll help you prep for launch while you call Chris and get a bead on that boat. You need to get the hell out of here."

You got that right.

Brian called Chris, the team's communications specialist, and since they'd been tracking everything nearby via satellite, he'd quickly found the kidnappers yacht. By the time Brian had set the bearings on Jennifer's navigation system, Jason had finished preparing the boat for launch.

Jason untied the Zodiac and sped off into the sunrise as Brian maneuvered Jennifer's yacht out of port and punched it toward his future.

~~~

Brian's phone rang and he answered before the first ring had finished. "Agent Allen, this is Interim Director Fellows. Director Santiago has been compromised. This is a matter for the state Department now. Your orders are to stand down."

Like hell I will.

"Say again, sir?"

"I said stand down. We need to let the State Department handle this."

Whatever, douchebag.

"I'm sorry, sir. I can't read you clearly. I've been having some trouble with my phone."

The State Department will find the quickest way to lose her trail and leave her for dead. Fellows has been gunning for Santiago's job for years. Sorry, boys, I don't play politics.

"You're loud and clear, Agent Allen, and I know you can hear me just fine. If you don't stand down, you'll be relieved of duty immediately."

How will you relieve me if you can't call me?

"You're still garbled, sir. Please relay your message through my handler."

And go fuck yourself.

Chapter 12

Jennifer listened at the door as Gary spoke to one of the kidnappers in the hallway.

"I told you. This is going to be a piece of cake. I made the phone call. We'll have our money in forty-eight hours, tops."

They already made a deal? How'd they show proof of life?

"Why don't you let me in on a few more details. It seems I'm the one taking all the risks here. Nobody said anything about bodyguards."

What?

Gary's voice pitched upwards. "I told you. She doesn't have bodyguards!"

"Then how do you explain those two fellas with hand cannons in a Zodiac?"

Hand cannons? Papa must have sent someone.

"That was probably just her new divers or, more logically, two guys who planned to do the same thing we're doing. We are talking ten...er... two million dollars here."

He's trying to short the muscle.

"Ten million?"

"Did I say ten? No, it's two. I'm dreaming of ten. I'd love to get ten, but we'll probably only get two for her."

"I think I should do the pickup when it's time. We wouldn't want anyone recognizing you."

"That's not the plan. I do the pickup. It's not negotiable."

Oh, shit. Gary isn't even in charge here. He just thinks he is.

"Everything is negotiable, Gary. Even life itself is negotiable."

"What's that supposed to mean? Just be careful how you treat her from now on. They'll want proof of life and we don't need her any more banged up than she already is. You got that, tough guy?"

That's telling him...not.

"Yeah, I got it. I won't bang up her face anymore, but that doesn't mean I can't have a little fun with her until the payoff."

"No, that's exactly what it means. She needs to be delivered undamaged." Gary turned the key in the lock and let himself into Jennifer's cabin.

Jennifer stepped from behind the door and didn't waste any time starting her interrogation as soon as he closed it. "I'm just curious, Gary, did my father put you up to this?"

If he didn't, you're in a world of shit.

"That's a stupid question. Your father has nothing to do with this." He sneered at her.

Not as stupid as you think.

"In that case, I'm sorry for you, Gary. I'm really sorry, because there isn't much chance of you coming out of this alive."

"Blah, blah, blah." He raised his hand for her to stop talking. "Whatever, bitch. I want my fucking payoff. I want cash in pocket! If you aren't letting me in on this dive, then I'll get my money one way or another where I can. I know your investors have you insured for kidnap and ransom, so the way I see it, I'll just take my money now without having to put up with you or do any heavy lifting of buried treasure. It's a much better deal that way."

"So it's all about the money?" She couldn't resist the dig. "Not a damaged pride thing?" She pursed her lips and crooked her finger to represent his flaccid member. He deserved the jab.

He narrowed his eyes and locked his jaw for a moment. "I've been waiting for you to pay off for two years now, and it's all been research, preparation and planning. You've got to dot all the I's and cross all the t's before you even make a step."

It's archaeology, not piracy, dumbass.

"It's called research for a reason, asshole."

"I don't care what you want to call it. I call it fear of living."

"You're a real piece of shit, you know that, Gary?

"Maybe, but I'll be a rich piece of shit in a couple days."

You'll be dead in a couple days.

She smiled and shook her head. "Nope. My father will kill you first."

He laughed like a man who didn't have a care. "Whatever. Just because your father runs a successful import and export business doesn't mean he has jack for pull in my world."

Your world?

"Gary, you poor stupid bastard. You have no idea who my father is, do you?"

"Unless he's Arnold Schwarzeneggar, I couldn't care less."

"Hmph. Arnold Schwarzeneggar couldn't even get an appointment with my father."

"Yeah, whatever."

She walked up to Gary and stood toe to toe with him, placing her hands on his shoulders. She spoke quietly so the man outside wouldn't hear. If he did, this would all go sideways in minutes. "Gary, you listen, and you listen good because you won't want me to say this loudly or more than once. My guess is your buddies out there won't be too happy when they find out." She spoke slowly as one might to a child. "My father is the Director of the Special Activities Division of the Central Intelligence Agency."

Gary's face went white. "C-come again?" He squeaked.

"My father imports and exports state secrets. He has an army of spies and assassins who have been recruited from the best military special forces teams in the United States, people who are probably at this very moment, planning for your immediate annihilation."

No joke. You're fucked.

Gary shook her hands off his shoulders and stepped back. "Nice fairy tale. Keep dreaming, princess."

He thinks I'm bluffing. I never bluff.

"Didn't you ever wonder why I had a scrambler for secure calls on my phone?"

She watched his face as Gary slowly started putting it all together.

The skin around his face and neck turned slightly green, and he swallowed hard.

"Yes, that's a lot for one tiny brain like yours to wrap itself around. Why don't you go take a walk and think about what we've discussed. Google "Florio Santiago". While you're at it, think about how your new best friends are going to feel when they find out you're all about to have a bunch of spooks crawling up your asses, and there will be no payday."

His pupils dilated as the thought registered, and she knew he finally understood what a world of hurt he'd stumbled into.

Eureka!

"Go away, Gary. I don't want you in here when you shit your pants and then cry like a little bitch because the end is nearer than you ever dreamed."

~~~

Jennifer watched as Gary walked slowly out of her cabin looking dazed. He locked the door behind him. His footfalls on the stairs didn't sound nearly as enthusiastic as they had been before. They sounded more like a man walking to the gallows – and he was.

If Papa didn't sanction this snatch and grab, Gary won't live to see another dawn.

She heard a click and her door opened. The big goon walked in smiling.

Did he hear us?

"It looks like we've got some time to wait before the ransom pickup, so I thought it was time we get to know each other a little better."

Gary didn't call it off?

Jennifer shook her head. "I don't think that's such a good idea. A good idea would be to drop me in the ocean and just walk away from this."

"And miss a two million dollar payday? No."

Somebody has got to have a brain cell in this operation! "Gary didn't tell you, did he?"

"Tell me what? That you're not to be touched? Yeah, but he ain't the boss, girlie." He crossed the cabin in two steps and grabbed her shoulders. "No phones or knives this time. No interruptions at all." He bent to kiss her hard, his tongue forcing its entry into her mouth."

No!

She managed to control her disgust long enough to bite the nasty invader.

The goon yelped and threw her against the wall.

Her vision blurred and she bit back the pain in her shoulder. She recovered quickly and came back punching hard and fast.

With a roar, he swung his arm and his fist made hard contact with her jaw.

"Stop it! Stop it now!" Gary stormed into the cabin during the struggle. "You can't do this. Why can't you just leave her the fuck alone? Do you know who her father is?"

"What the fuck do I care? She ain't my daughter." He rubbed his crotch and laughed in her direction.

Disgusting pig.

"Shut up, you stupid asshole." Gary was waving his arms in a panicky frenzy now. "You can't do this!"

"Why the hell not? She's mine until they buy her back."

More like you're mine.

"Shit. I can't do this. I can't be a part of this." Gary sat in the small chair by the sink and rocked back and forth. "Tell him who your father is, Jennifer."

Jennifer wiped the blood from her mouth with the back of her wrist. "My father is Florio Santiago, Director of the Special Activities Division of the Central Intelligence Agency."

The meathead's bloody smile fell as the corners of Jennifer's mouth turned upward into a grin.

Shit. It hurts when I smile.

"This would end better for all of you if you just dropped me at the nearest port and forgot you ever saw me. I don't think he'll be coming to get me personally, but I would imagine some of his associates will be relieving you of your burden shortly. Be nice and maybe Daddy will let you live. I hear they have lovely accommodations at Guantanamo Bay."

The big man swallowed. He looked as though he were trying to process all the information she just threw at him.

Probably got a mouth full of blood from where I bit you, eh champ?

He rubbed his chin and stared at Jennifer for a long moment as she held her breath. He'd probably kill her now. Gary was likely hoping that was the next move.

What a prick.

Jennifer waited for the inevitable in silence. Gentle waves rocked the boat, making it all very dreamlike. The air was still, and she was suddenly acutely aware of her own heartbeat. Did they hear it too?

Movements seemed to happen in slow motion.

The man Gary thought he controlled moved his hand down his side to his holster and unsnapped the trigger guard. His eyes never left hers.

Her life, all the things she'd accomplished, and the many things she'd never had the chance to do, flashed like a silent movie through her mind as he pulled his handgun from the holster and leveled it at her head.

This was it. It made sense. That's what she'd do if she'd ever been caught in such an untenable situation.

Of course, I'd never be so stupid as to not know my mark.

She took a deep breath, closed her eyes and prepared for the bullet. Off in the distance, she thought she heard a boat motor coming toward them. Not just any boat, but her boat.

Wishful thinking.

Blackness.

Chapter 13

Lightning strikes of pain shot through Jennifer's head every time she opened her eyes.

I'm alive!

She finally stopped trying to open her eyes, focusing on the ache in her right shoulder and elbow. She stretched her arm tentatively and smiled as she realized it wasn't broken.

Something dripped down her cheek as she lay there. She wiped at it and opened her eyes, holding them open long enough to see fresh blood. Her nose was bleeding. She felt it with her left hand to see if it might be broken. No, she knew she'd feel much more pain if it were broken.

Bracing her hands on the edge of the small bunk, she stood up slowly, conscious of the painful throbbing in her head and took the short step to the sink. She breathed a silent sigh of relief at the fact she had some running water. Splashing some water on her face, she rinsed the blood away. She grabbed the dingy, old washcloth by the sink, rinsed it and pinched her bleeding nose with it. Leaning against the wall, she tipped her head back to stop the flow from her nose.

They didn't kill me. What now?

Footsteps made their way down the stairs and stopped outside her cabin door. "Is she awake?"

Her blood ran cold at the sound of Gary's voice. Her stomach turning with the very thought of him.

"Yeah, man. I heard her run the water. No tears yet. She's a tough bird."

I'll show you a tough bird, peckerhead.

"About that...you weren't supposed to hurt her."

Oh, that's rich. He sets her up to be kidnapped by thugs and actually thinks they'll be gentle?

"You don't make the rules, now do you? We're running this show."

The hairs on the back of Jennifer's neck stood up at the confident, menacing lilt in his voice. Gary was in over his head. She knew it, but did he?

"I set this thing up. I'm the reason you're going to make a very large sum of money."

Gary always did think he was more important than he actually was.

"Riiiight." He dragged out the word. "What did you say the split was again?"

Jennifer knew that tone. She'd heard it before from others. It meant someone was going to get cut out of the deal.

Careful, Gary.

"I get half and you get half. A million each. For a million bucks you'd think you could at least see the goods don't get damaged."

Jennifer knew that Gary was well aware her kidnap and ransom insurance covered up to ten million.

You're shorting the muscle by four million. I wonder how they'd feel if they knew?

"Except the crew pay has to come out of my half. I think now is a good time to renegotiate."

"Renegotiate? No way! We had a deal, fifty-fifty. I brought you this opportunity on a silver platter."

Is he whining? What an amateur.

"So you refuse to renegotiate?"

This can't go well.

"Wait. What are you--?" Gary's voice wavered. "There's no need for that. Of...of course we can talk about this."

She'd heard him scared once, after a close call with a great white. His voice shook now like it had then.

A single gunshot echoed through the corridor, followed by a thunk against the door of her cabin.

Jennifer jumped and gasped, covering her mouth quickly. She crossed to the bunk carefully so as not to draw attention from the kidnapper outside.

Oh my God. He shot Gary. I'm next.

"That was an unacceptable counteroffer, man. Looks like I get a hundred percent." Footsteps faded away down the hall.

What do I do now?

She sat tentatively on the small bed, staring at the cabin door as a dark red stain slowly seeped under it.

Gary was dead out there. This simple kidnapping just got very complicated.

Tears of frustration welled in her eyes as she realized just how desperate her situation was. Cold and loneliness surrounded her as she considered her situation.

I've got to find a way off this boat now!

~~~

Brian tread water close to the hull of the kidnappers' boat as he inspected the charge. He placed it just below the waterline in the bow. It would only create a hole big enough to make the boat list to port so they'd have to evacuate. In the confusion after the explosion they'd be so busy trying to figure out what was going on in the bow that they'd completely forget about the hostage they had in the stern. The surprise would make his extraction of Jennifer all the easier. If he couldn't board during the initial confusion, he could pick the kidnappers off once they got on a lifeboat and then grab Jennifer.

Simple operation. In and out, and nobody will ever find your bodies.

He checked his watch. Brian looked around and took a deep breath before diving. The pop of a flare gun broke the stillness, and he paused to see where it had come from.

What the hell?

Three feet of the stern of the boat blew off in a loud explosion. Surprise at the explosion and the force of the pressure from it hitting him pushed the breath out of his lungs.

The entire engine area had been blown off the stern.

Jennifer!

The boat wasn't going to list slowly, it was going down hard and fast, like a stone. A fireball of a man wailed as he jumped into the water.

What the hell is going on?

Remembering his own charge that had risen out of reach as the stern sank, Brian's instincts told him to swim as fast as he could away from the sinking yacht that would soon suck everything nearby, including him and Jennifer, down with it. He looked toward the gaping wound in the wreckage. If she'd been knocked unconscious, he'd only have a few moments to get her to the surface. Even though something in his gut told him she wouldn't be there, he dove anyway.

The boat fell quickly toward the shallow bottom, and Brian swam directly into it. Swimming into a sinking boat wasn't on his top ten list of fun things to do, but he had to know where Jennifer was.

The kidnappers had been anchored offshore, but if someone heard the explosion, they could be poking around with police at any minute. Time was of the essence.

He swam through the huge hole and into the wreckage. He made his way to the cabin where he knew they'd held Jennifer. It was an old boat, and the kidnappers were sloppy about security, so he was able to do a complete recon of the boat during the night without being detected.

Jesus, Jennifer. Where are you?

He tried her cabin door, but it was jammed. Furniture could have fallen against it. He braced himself against the opposite wall and pressed his feet against the door, exerting all his might to extend his legs through and open the door. It still wouldn't open. He took a deep breath from his oxygen tank for a final push. The door still wouldn't budge.

Time was running out for Jennifer. If she didn't have air, she'd be buried in there. Taking one more deep breath, he swam out through the gaping wound and around the outside of the boat to the porthole. The vessel had sunk now, raising a cloud of debris from the bottom. Sand and dirt blurred his vision as he swam to the porthole.

It's open!

He poked his head inside and looked around. She wasn't there.

She got out!

Bubbles rose as he laughed.

I'll bet she finally shot someone with a flare gun and is happily swimming toward shore by now.

Brian pushed off the wreckage and made his way to the surface as quickly as he could.

He came up for air, breathing deeply as he scanned the waterline between him and the shore. Yes, there she was, swimming toward shore.

Damn, she's moving fast!

"Jennifer!" Tearing into the water, Brian gave it all he had to catch her before she made land. Once she hit solid ground, she'd be vulnerable. She'd have the sense to hide from her kidnappers, but that would also make it more difficult for Brian to find her. He couldn't afford to waste time.

Every several strokes, he looked up to see where she was and shout her name. She'd make shore before he caught up with her.

Damnit!

The tourist hotels and busy beaches on the coast of Bizerte wouldn't make looking for her easy. If she was smart, and Brian now understood that she was, she'd do whatever she could to mix in as soon as possible and then get lost in a crowd.

Chapter 14

Jennifer finally found footing on the sandy beach and tried not to bring too much attention to herself. She'd headed for the large hotel and made it just to the edge of the resort's beach area. Hopefully any one of the vacationing Europeans would think she was just a tourist who took a dip in her clothes.

A pair of shorts and a tiny tee shirt, both wet. Good thing nobody is paying any attention to me.

She knew she needed fresh clothes to mix in and get to the nearest embassy. The cops in this part of the world were notoriously dirty.

It's okay, girl. Just channel Bo Derek. You can do it. Walk up the beach like you own it.

She walked up to an umbrella with two empty chaises cluttered with the standard tourist items. A beach bag, sunglasses, water bottles… She slipped on the sunglasses, grabbed a bottle of water and snatched the beach bag on her way by.

Don't look at me. These things are mine. I did not just wash up on the beach. I'm not the illegal alien you're looking for.

She tucked in through the side door of the huge white hotel beyond the umbrellas and chaises. She breathed a sigh of relief when she saw a ladies' room just inside. Locking the door behind her, she set the beach bag down to rifle through the contents. The first thing she looked for was something to tell her where she was. A hotel key and a local brochure told her she was at a beach resort in Tunisia. Next out of the bag, she pulled a large piece of beige cloth.

A sheet? Really?

As she pulled the large piece out, she realized it was an overgarment the Muslim women wore in Northern Africa, a sefseri, and thanked God for her luck. She wrapped it around herself as best she could, careful to cover her legs as much as possible while still covering her hair and crossing a corner over her face. She looked at herself in the mirror.

Yes, I might just manage to make the embassy in Tunis. Now I just need a ride. This would be so much easier if I could just call Dad. Getting a call through to a Director at the CIA from a phone in Tunisia? Hah!

She'd have better luck stealing a car and making a run for the Embassy. From there, they could call her father and straighten all this out. He was probably worried already since she'd missed her usual daily check in.

She checked the bag for anything else. A romance novel was all that was left.

The Path to Freedom? Irony, or a light at the end of the tunnel? Damn, no shoes or car keys.

She took small, quick steps so her bare feet wouldn't show as she walked through the main lobby. Gunshots startled her as they rang out from the direction of the beach.

Did they manage to follow me? I've got to get out of here, now!

A little brown fiat pulled up in front of the hotel and the driver jumped out, leaving it running as he bolted into the lobby shouting a guest's name.

Panicked guests, wide eyed and shouting, flooded the lobby. She kept her gaze down and ran for the car still running in the portico.

Thank you!

She scrambled through the front doors quickly and lunged into the driver's seat of the Fiat. She closed the door and jammed the little car into gear. She realized women didn't often drive in these parts and she'd quickly stand out. She turned out of the parking lot, switched gears and drove off as quickly as possible without squealing the tires. When she made her way into city traffic, she looked for signs leading to Tunis. If she had enough gas she could make it to the embassy and contact her father from there.

She considered calling him now, but she could still hear gunfire in the distance. This whole area was too dangerous. Police would be blocking traffic soon and she had no money or identification. These people weren't exactly the kind to lend a hand when a strange American dropped in and asked for help.

No, stay in the car. Get to Tunis and go to the embassy. Being detained now could last a lifetime. The embassy is the safest place to be.

Besides, it would be too embarrassing to explain that she'd been kidnapped because she'd emasculated an employee, and now she'd washed up on a foreign shore with no clothes and no money. That was a scandal her father would never forgive her for!

No, the best thing to do is to get to the embassy, then pay the owner of the car for their trouble from the safety of a wire transfer.

~~~

Brian shed his wetsuit before walking up on the beach, barefoot and carrying a small black pack. He slipped his earpiece in and grabbed his phone from the pack. "Dial Santiago." He commanded the phone.

Santiago answered his private line.

"I don't have much time. I lost her. Track my cellphone for coordinates."

"Excuse me?" Florio Santiago's voice had a note of incredulity. "How could you lose her?"

Brian couldn't blame him. The whole thing was pretty crazy. He pulled a pair of shoes from the small pack and slipped them on. "I overheard them talking about how much trouble she was going to be and how they were going to make her disappear and avoid the hassle." He left his handgun in the pack and slung it over his shoulder as he stood.

"Jesus."

Brian ran up the beach toward the hotel. "I figured that was reason enough to go in, so I planned a little distraction. I figured I could get in and get her out before they noticed."

"And by distraction, you mean explosion."

"Naturally."

"Naturally." The Director groaned. "Agent Allen, I'm looking at the satellite image. The boat was destroyed. That was more than a little distraction. If you killed my daughter, so help me God, I will rain down hell so hard on you--"

Brian grinned as he jogged up to the entrance he'd seen Jennifer go through. "She's fine and yes, sir, it was a big explosion, but in all fairness, I wasn't responsible for all of it."

"You weren't responsible for all of it? A little bit destroyed is like being a little bit pregnant. Blowing up boats is your goddamned trademark!"

"Why thank you, sir. I do pride myself on that."

"Allen, focus."

"I am sir, but you are a bit of a distraction." Sandy footprints led to the ladies room. "Jennifer?" He opened the door to find it empty. "Shit."

"Shit? Speak to me with full sentences, Allen."

She was good but she's in the wind.

He was finding more reasons to admire this woman every day. "Sir, I blew a hole in that boat so it would sink slowly. There was a second, unrelated explosion in the stern. That one I can't take credit for. I don't know who rigged it to go up in a fireball."

"Jesus Christ!" Santiago was really wound up now. "Who did it? Is there somebody else involved in this circus now?"

"Yes, sir. From what I could gather," Brian chuckled, "It was your daughter that sank that boat like a brick."

"Ay, Maria! That girl's as much trouble as her mother. Do you have her now?"

"No, sir."

Small arms fire rang out on the beach. Brian ran back to the entrance and took a quick look out the window. Armed men were sweeping the beach. Jennifer was nowhere to be seen. Besides, her sandy footprints continued down the hall.

"Is that gunfire?"

He'd almost forgotten Santiago was still on the line. "Not my monkeys. Not my circus. I'll call you when I find Jennifer."

"Damnit. She's as independent and bullheaded..." His words trailed off. There was a sort of growl that morphed into a roar on the other end of the phone line. "She has just enough experience to be dangerous. She'd know to get to the embassy. Look for her there or on her way there."

"Already ahead of you. I'm about to catch a ride now." Brian strode quickly through the pandemonium in the lobby and made his way to the parking lot. An older model Mercedes was ripe for the picking. He got in and hotwired it as quickly as he might light a match.

This is why spies have handlers. These desk jockeys talk to much.

"I'll let the embassy know you're on your way. How far behind are you?"

"I estimate no more than five minutes. Let me know if she gets in touch with you."

"I will. Go find my daughter, Allen, before she gets herself into any more trouble."

"Yes, sir."

Brian hung up, slipped the car into gear and drove as quickly as he could out of the parking lot and into the city traffic. He chuckled as he thought about Jennifer.

She has balls. That girl is no shrinking violet. How many other women would know to make their escape like she had?

He scanned the road as he drove, checking his watch along the way. She must have been picked up because he was already close to Tunis and hadn't seen her anywhere on the road. He searched for taxis in front of him.

A lump stuck in his gut.

She should have been easy to spot, soaking wet on the side of the road.

Yeah, a beautiful Latina woman with those legs, soaking wet on the side of the road.

He snapped back to reality as a van skidded between his car and the sloped shoulder of the road. It was driving too fast and reckless even for this road.

She doesn't stand a chance in hell. Somebody's going to pick her up if they haven't already.

The windows in the van looked blacked out. His stomach knotted as he considered the possibility she'd been seen and picked up by Tunisians who shared the Muslim worldview that infidel women should be used as slaves and concubines. Brian didn't want to think about the slavers who might have snagged her.

Maybe she stole a car?

Chapter 15

"Fuck!" Jennifer cursed out loud.

Steam rose so thick from the radiator that she had to pull over before the whole thing blew. She only had a couple more kilometers to Tunis. She could do it on foot easily if she had shoes. Barefoot was a whole different story.

She searched the back seat for something she could wrap her feet with. A couple rags left on the floorboard would have to do. She ripped strips and wrapped them around her feet. Traffic was slowing, and the sun was going down. With any luck she could slip into Tunis unnoticed and find her way to the embassy.

She waited until she couldn't see any cars coming up behind her and stepped out of the car, quickly walking in her makeshift rag shoes.

They aren't so bad, really.

She remembered the time she cut her feet on a coral reef and was grateful for the rags between her and the gravel today. She'd left a trail of blood walking through the sand after diving that day.

She smiled under the stifling sefseri. She'd make it to the embassy by hook or by crook. She'd already escaped her kidnappers, and would be back on her own boat soon. She wasn't usually happy about her father's position in the CIA, but she was today.

He can clear my identity with the embassy and get me on my way back to Morocco. With any luck, I may only lose a few days on my timetable.

She kept her head down and checked the sefseri to be sure she was covered. Just as she picked up her pace, a car pulled up behind her and a cloud of dust overtook her.

No, don't pull over for me. Just keep driving.

Chills ran through her body.

Something isn't right about this.

She pressed the sefseri against her nose and mouth to filter the dust and kept moving forward.

It could be a rescue or it could be trouble. Most likely trouble.

A man shouted in Arabic. Her heart raced. A rescuer would have tried English first.

This could be bad.

She quickened her step and shook her head.

He shouted again and she heard a car door open as she widened the gap between them.

A sign on the roadside cheered her. Tunis was only half a kilometer. Once she was there, she could find the embassy easily enough and be home free.

She heard the crunch of gravel as the van rolled up slowly behind her.

Too close.

A woman's voice called to her in Arabic. She turned and said "No, thank you", careful to mimic the woman's dialect as best she could. It was a small van. The woman insisted she ride with her. "Poor child with rags on your feet. The road is not safe. Come ride with us."

I should have looked for a weapon in that car. At least a tire iron.

Everything about this good Samaritan felt wrong, and Jennifer shook her head and picked up her pace. She heard the door close and sighed.

The van continued crushing the gravel, slowly, inching up behind her.

Cold fear and panic washed over her.

She scanned the ground for a stick or a rock, something, anything, to make her not feel so helpless. There was nothing. Beads of sweat tickled down her spine like icy fingers.

The van's engine revved as it rolled up beside her. The side door slid open and the woman motioned her inside.

Jennifer shook her head and broke into a run.

A man jumped out of the passenger side and grabbed her.

She dropped the corner of the sefseri covering her face and punched him hard in the nose.

Before she could recover from the impact and run, he grunted and slapped her full force and threw her into the van, jumping in on top of her as the van sped into traffic.

Jennifer struggled, but the man was pressing against her with his full weight. She struggled and gasped for breath under his weight.

Something ripped as she screamed, kicked and bit.

No! Not this! Not again! What are the fucking odds?!

Duct tape was slapped over her mouth and her nostrils flared with deep panicked breaths.

There was more ripping as the man rolled her onto her side and the woman taped her wrists behind her back.

No matter how accomplished she became in her field, no matter how far from The Farm she roamed, the same fate seemed to follow her.

Captured. Vulnerable. A victim. I will not be a victim!

The man sat her up against the van wall and she managed one good kick to his groin. He doubled over with a groan and she kicked wildly at his head.

The woman was screaming something too fast to be intelligible and looked pretty pissed off.

What's that in her hand? A fucking syringe!

Jennifer shook her head vigorously in a bid for mercy. "No, no!" She mumbled through the tape.

"Don't move." The woman spoke in Arabic as she prepared the syringe.

The man had recovered, somewhat. He punched Jennifer in the stomach. The excessive force of his punch confirmed the effectiveness of her kick.

She choked through the tape as the wind blew out of her and tears welled in her eyes. She blinked them back.

The man took a closer look at her. The fabric of her cover had come loose in the scuffle and her T-shirt and shorts we're now visible. He smiled and spoke in Arabic. "Look what we have here, mother."

The old woman squinted at her as she flicked the air bubbles from the syringe. "European?"

"She'll get a good price! This is wonderful."

They have no idea I understand Arabic.

"Yes, she might be worth the trouble at the end of the day."

You've got to be shitting me! Of all the fucking luck! I kick Gary out and get kidnapped. The negotiators stall for time and leave me to my own devices. Then I manage to be my own hero and blow the engine on the boat holding me and escape, only to crawl up onto a beach and get kidnapped by someone else? What the fuck are the odds?

She snorted through the duct tape.

How do I get out of this now?

For a moment she entertained a twinge of rage as she considered how easy it would have been for her father to have her rescued from the first kidnappers, but somehow Brian's number was the redial.

Of all the shit luck.

After everything I tried to do for papa, he was never there when I needed him. Why would he be now? She'd gone through the recruiting program for the Agency. She came through all the tests at the Farm with flying colors, but that asshat with a hard on for her father thought it would be a good idea to kidnap and torture her. That career was over before it started.

She leaned her head back against the bare metal wall of the van. She was deep in it now. She had no doubt the milky white substance in the syringe was an opiate. She was too exhausted from the swimming, the running, and the scuffle in the van to put up any more of a fight. She gritted her teeth and breathed deeply as the man held her down and the woman shot the warm liquid into her thigh.

~~~

Brian followed the van at a safe distance as it drove into Tunis.

The broken down car a few clicks up the road, the erratic driving, all stunk. He ran all the possibilities through his head as he drove, but one stuck. Jennifer had found a car, it broke down, then she got picked up, probably forcibly, by the people who owned the van, and likely gave then hell while they bound and gagged her.

He dialed Santiago's number.

"Did you find her?"

"I've got a hunch. I need a satellite."

"I can't give you a satellite on a hunch."

"With all due respect, sir, you need to be in this or out. If you want to see your daughter again, you'd better think of a good reason to get a satellite, because I think I've been made and these people are about to get away with her."

"Okay, what are we tracking?"

"A white Sherpa van, two cars ahead of my location. Let me know where it goes and then get me the address of a safe house. I'm going to need to get some hardware."

"All right, I'm tracking you now. I'll get an agent to follow the van with a satellite. He'll call you with an address when it stops. My secretary will send you the safe house address. Give me some hope here, Allen. Can you see Jennifer?"

"No, sir. But I'm certain she's in that van."

"You'd better be right. The safe house is expecting you. This just went up to an international incident. I'm not sure how much more help I can expect from Fellows."

"Yes, sir. I understand. We'll get her back."

"I know you will, Agent Allen."

The car lurched, metal crunched, and Brian's phone flew out the open window as he spun once, twice, and then his tires hit the soft shoulder of the road and the car tumbled, side over side, into a deep wash. He watched as it all seemed to happen in slow motion. He'd been distracted while he was driving and a taxi had sideswiped him as he was focused on the van.

I'm usually better than that.

The taxi driver had waved an insult at him just before the spinning began. He'd need to get out of this car and get a new one quickly.

I'll never catch up with the van. At least they're tracking her with satellite now.

His biggest problem right now was that he'd never find another secure phone. The safe house would be compromised if he lost his phone and someone else found it. Would he be conscious when the car finally stopped tumbling? Too many thoughts raced through his head as he seemed to roll down the hill in slow motion.

Adrenaline pumped through his veins with every bass beat of his heart. He knew he had to get out of the car, up the hill and find his phone before someone else did. The security was high-speed on the phone, but any hacker worth his salt would find a way in with enough time.

The car slid to a sudden stop and he landed crumpled in a heap in what should have been the roof over the back seat. The vehicle came to rest upside down. The windows had been open and he took a moment to smile in gratitude at not having been tossed from the vehicle as it rolled down the ravine.

Thank you Jesus for dumb luck!

He shimmied out the window facing the wash, just in case there was someone up on the road, gunning for him. He looked up and scanned the hill. Nobody was there. There was only the sound of more cars whizzing by as they all raced to their destinations.

He scrambled up the long hill. His bag had flown out the window at some point and was nowhere to be seen. When he finally made it to the side of the road, beaten, bruised and covered with sweat and dirt, he stopped, took a deep breath, and a physical inventory.

Nothing broken. Ten clicks to Tunis. I can run there.

Something hard hit his shin with a crack.

Son of a bitch!

Had a passing truck thrown a rock? He bent to rub his shin.

Sweet baby Jesus! My phone!

Somehow the phone had been thrown by the tire of a passing truck. He picked it up and the case had held. Then the phone rang.

It still works!

"Allen, we've identified the building the van went to. You were right, she probably got picked up by slavers. The embassy hasn't seen her yet and nobody has left that building since the van drove into the compound."

"Great. I'm going tactical as soon as I can arm up."

"No, finesse it. Security is heightened after that attack on the beach. Going in guns-a-blazing will only cause more trouble and place both of you in even more danger. We've got an asset there who can make an introduction to the right people. You need to appear to be a wealthy buyer or they won't talk to you."

Brian looked down at his filthy shorts and tee shirt. "Sure... I can pull that off."

With a minor miracle.

"The asset will contact you shortly."

"Great." Brian hung up and looked down at his banged up phone case and torn, dirty clothes. They had been nice once upon a time, but sea water, filthy roads, getting washed up on shore, stealing cars, and all the other excitement had taken their toll. Not to mention getting bounced around in a car that was pushed off a road into a dry, dusty wash.

"Gonna need a little backup on this one." Brian punched the speed dial and started running.

Jason answered. "How goes the side job, brother? Is waitressing all you thought it would be?"

"Listen, Jase, I need a cover ID and everything else that goes along with being wealthy enough to buy a slave on the black market."

"Oh, snap. Some guys get all the luck. Wait a second. She got taken by slavers? The Director's daughter got kidnapped by slavers? Holy fuck, dude. Hold on, okay, you're on speaker. Go, for Will."

Will's voice came across loud and clear. "Sitrep?"

"We've located her. I have to look like a player, complete with walking around cash. I need clothes, money, shoes, bling, and I need them yesterday."

"Are you running?"

"Yeah. Wrecked my Mercedes a couple clicks back."

"You're 1300 clicks away." Will paused.

"I'm running to Tunis, not Morocco."

"Shut up. I need to do the math."

Brian knew better than to interrupt Will when he was putting a plan together, so he waited on the line, oblivious to traffic as he continued to run along the side of the road into Tunis, focused on his destination and putting a plan together before he got there.

"That's way out of chopper range, and the G6 would still take six or seven hours to get there. We'll have to wire the money to the embassy and you'll have to shop local."

"Not a problem. When can you get me the money?"

"I'm having Chris transfer one hundred thousand now."

Chris' voice chimed in. "Brian, they'll have it at the embassy for you within the hour."

"Great." He checked his watch. "I should be there in a few minutes. Call ahead for me. I don't look so respectable right now."

"Chris anticipated that and put in a call to Mr. Coty. He's our man there."

"You need backup?" Jason chimed in, clearly itching for a fix of action. "I can be there tonight with the G6, help your cover a little?"

"That's a good idea," Will agreed. "Sarah and Jay are staying here a few days so we'll put everything we can into your operation. I'll send Jason with the jet."

Brian smiled. It would be good to have Jason around as backup if things went sideways again. Jason worked best in chaos so this was right up his alley. "You sure you can spare him, Chief?"

A car honked at Brian as he dodged a large rock on the side of the road.

"It'll be a hardship, but I think he needs the break. Besides, you'll need to get her back here ASAP, and the jet will be the best way to do that after what she's been through. You still running?"

"Yeah. Thanks, man."

"No sweat. Watch your six."

"Not funny. Wilco." Brian clicked off and slowed his pace as he came closer to the guard house outside the embassy. He raised his hands. "Special Agent Brian Allen. Mr. Coty is expecting me."

Section 20

Chapter 16

Spending his summers in Saudi Arabia as a kid had prepared Brian for operations in the Middle East. He understood Arab culture and that included shopping, which was done completely differently than back in the U.S.A. After a few hours with a tailor and a couple more drinking chai with a jeweler, Brian's shopping was complete and he still had plenty of cash in the event these dirtbag slavers tried to high-ball him.

He looked in the mirror.

Not bad. Millionaire buyer from the United States? Sure.

A knock at the door reminded him of the time. He answered the door.

"Mr. Allen?"

"Yes. And you are?"

"Karim Haddad. It's a pleasure to meet you."

Karim Haddad, the asset, had made the arrangements for Brian to meet the slavers tonight.

After a short exchange, Karim drove Brian to the compound.

Brian examined every detail as they drove up and waited for the gates to open. He couldn't go tactical on this place alone if they had any guards. It was a veritable fortress. He checked his watch. Jason should be landing soon.

After parking in the courtyard, they were ushered into a sitting room with bright carpets on the floor and low sofas. The elderly man who greeted them bid them to have a seat. "Would you care for a drink, sir?"

"Chai, thank you."

"Please be seated. Mister Hazim will join you in just a moment." He motioned to a sofa and disappeared into another room.

Brian and Karim sat on either end of the sofa.

"Good evening, Mr. Allen." The middle-aged man in a grey silk suit was all charm as he reached to shake Brian's hand. "I am Hazim. I trust your trip here went well?"

Avoiding a chat on how he'd blown up a boat, washed up on shore and rode a totaled car down into a ravine, Brian stood, replied politely and shook the man's hand. "Yes, very well. Thank you."

Hazim sat in one of the club chairs facing the sofa while Brain and Karim sat back down. "May I offer you a cigar?" Hazim motioned to the humidor on the low table in front of the sofa.

Brian smiled politely. "Thank you, no."

The butler entered the room with an ornate tray of gold chai glasses, and a hot pot of tea.

Brian took the glass he offered. "Thank you."

Hazim insisted on more small talk. "So are you here on business, or simply pleasure?"

As frustrating as it was, Brian understood it was the custom. "My business keeps me close, but I'm here strictly for pleasure tonight."

"My friend, Karim, tells me you're looking for something specific. A Latina, I believe?"

Brian smiled. "Yes, I'm particularly fond of them."

"You do understand that we are a by-order only service? Latina's are difficult to come by. I could take an order and let you know when we have one."

"Ah." Brian set his chai on the table. "I was under the impression you could accommodate tonight."

"Sadly, I cannot. I do have a Latina but she's already spoken for. We have many nice girls. I'm sure you'll see something you like. I'll have them brought out."

"That's very generous, thank you, but I had my mind set on a Latina. I'm sure you understand. It's my preference."

"Of course. Most of our clients have very specific preferences, but I'm sorry. We have had an order for one for weeks, and she finally landed in our lap, so to speak." He paused as he eyed Brian. "You look like a man of means. Perhaps if you would like to attend our auction, we might come to an arrangement?"

Brian smiled and tilted his head slightly in deference. "Money isn't an object, but forgive my impertinence, time is."

Hazim smiled but Brian wasn't feeling it. "Of course." He scribbled something on a notepad and gave it to Karim. "We like to entertain on our boat. Please join us by midnight. You won't want to miss the show."

Karim accepted the slip of paper and then spoke in Arabic to Hazim. "I think Mister Allen might feel more assured of the opportunity if he could see the merchandise. Is she here? May we have a look at her?"

Hazim shook his head. "It's getting late and she's already on the boat, getting ready for the party." He snapped his fingers and the old manservant entered the room and handed him a cellphone. He offered it to Brian. "There she is, but we have some other excellent merchandise, as you can see. I think you'll be very impressed."

Brian looked at the photo and confirmed it was Jennifer. She was asleep or unconscious. He held back his anger and used his best poker face as he flipped through the rest of the photos. "My compliments, Hazim." He handed the phone back and smiled like a douchebag who was about to buy a kidnapped woman thrown into slavery through no fault of her own.

"We'll see you tonight then." Hazim nodded.

~~~

Jennifer woke to gentle brushstrokes on her face. She blinked several times before she could focus. Pain resonated throughout her body. There was so much of it that she couldn't pinpoint any one injury to focus on.

Someone was applying makeup to her face.

Jennifer tried to lick her lips, but her mouth was too dry. Waving the makeup woman off with a hand, she struggled to sit up. She blinked several times and looked around the room. There was no mistaking it was the cabin of a boat. Albeit a much nicer boat than the one she'd previously been held in. Several other women were in the room, being dressed and made up. Jennifer knew a human auction when she saw one.

Probably on a private yacht, well off the coast, loaded with a bunch of rich drunk men who would rather buy a slave than meet a woman the old fashioned way.

How do I get off this boat? I need to get up on deck.

She glanced around the room looking for anything she could use as a weapon, but despite all the makeup and brushes, she couldn't even see so much as a flat iron.

The woman who had been doing her makeup smiled. "They gave you too much. Here," she passed Jennifer a bottle of water, "drink this."

Jennifer took the water and drank as much as she could. "Thank you."

I've got to get hydrated and break this haze. I need to be able to move so I can get myself out of here.

Most of the other girls were docile and helping with their own makeup. Some of them might have been hookers hired for the party, but Jennifer focused on her own situation.

A man of medium build walked into the room. He didn't look terribly impressive as a bodyguard, but Jennifer caught a glance at a handgun tucked in the back of his belt.

Here's my chance.

He walked toward her and smiled.

She returned his smile. "Hi there." The closer she could get to him, the easier it would be to grab his weapon and turn the tables.

He spoke in Arabic to the woman doing her makeup. "She should pay off well." He grabbed her chin and turned her head slightly. "Get rid of that bruise. It'll make a few hundred Euros' difference."

Jennifer gently stroked his thigh and stood. It was a bold move but she needed that gun. She whispered in his ear in Arabic. "You could kiss it and make it better."

The moment he slid his right hand around her waist, she grabbed the gun. Her first shot was true and blew out his knee.

The women screamed and there was a flurry of makeup and lingerie as Jennifer ran for the door and ripped it open.

A man stood on the other side of it.

Her gun jammed.

Everything went black.

Chapter 17

Brian nodded to Jason as Karim parked the car in front of the dock. They'd be taxied to the auction yacht from there. "You'd better stay put, Karim. We'll take it from here."

"Thank you, Agent Allen." Karim seemed visibly relieved, and sighed.

"Ready, Jase?"

"Let's do this."

Brian and Jason walked to the boat that was waiting for them. "You sure this whole water taxi thing is a good idea?"

"Yeah. If Jennifer is on that boat, we're taking it and her with us tonight."

Jason shrugged. "So many yachts. So little time."

They were greeted on the yacht by Hazim and two girls who already looked drunk. Brian knew they were probably drugged. "Mister Allen. So good of you to come."

"Thank you for having us. This is my associate, Mister Williams. He's an enthusiast with deep pockets. I hope we didn't miss anything."

"I'm sorry, but due to the unexpected demand for a particular product, we couldn't keep it."

"I don't follow your meaning. You said it would be auctioned tonight."

Hazim took Brian aside and whispered to him. "That particular product was very difficult to keep. She was a troublemaker. We had to send her away."

"Away?"

"She wasn't top quality. We have a reputation for providing product of a particular disposition. She didn't meet our standards so we sent her by boat with several others to an associate in Odessa who specializes in that sort."

Brian shook his head. He needed to keep his cover but get the hell off this boat immediately. "Well, this has been a very disappointing trip, Hazim." He reached into his breast pocket and pulled out a card case. "I trust you'll call me when you have another Latina." He handed Hazim a business card and replaced the card case. Then he reached into his trouser pocket, retrieving a money clip.

"Of course, Mr. Allen. You'll be the first I call."

"Despite the lack of product, you've been very generous." He counted out five hundred dollars. "Thank you for your time and courtesy."

"Thank you, Mr. Allen."

Brian gave Jason a curt nod and Jason extracted himself from between the two women as they boarded the water taxi to go back to shore.

Brian passed the local man a hundred dollar bill. "There's another for you if you get us back quickly.

~~~

"So what's the play, Bri?"

"She wasn't there. They sent her to Odessa." "Why, when they could have sold her to you?"

Brian smiled. "Apparently she was too much trouble."

Jason chuckled. "That one is a spitfire!"

This was one break Brian planned to take advantage of. He and Jason's teammate, Sarah Stevens, was deep undercover in the Russian mob and owned all the arms and drug shipping action on the Mediterranean, and some in the Black Sea. He called Sarah from the safe house and she said she'd call some Russian friends to see what she could do.

Brian's phone rang ten minutes later.

Yes!

"Hey, Sarah. That was fast."

"Brian, I've got some bad news for you. The boat arrives in Odessa at noon and I can't get you into the auction. You have until noon to get on that freighter and get her before she disappears again."

"Aren't you just a little ray of sunshine? Any suggestions?" Sara knew all the shipping organizations, and owned a solid fleet of ships herself. If she couldn't stop the boat for him, it meant somebody in a rival organization owned it.

"Here's what I suggest. You and Jason fly into Mihail Kogalniceanu Airport. I'll have a car there to take you to the Hotel Iaki in Mamaia. Check in at the hotel."

"And take a little spa day? What the fuck, Sarah?"

"Shut up, putz. One of my people is taking care of the room now. He'll be sure to have plenty of equipment and hardware for the trip waiting for you. Once you've checked in an armed up, go down to the beach hut."

"And rent boogey boards? What is this, Austin Powers?"

"I understand you're invested in this. Do you want my help or would you prefer to do this yourself?"

"Continue."

"I will have a boatman waiting for you. He'll take you as close as he can to the cargo ship under cover of night. The rest is up to you. Will that work?"

Brian laughed. "And that was just a suggestion? That's excellent, Sarah. Thanks for your help. Sorry about the sarcasm."

"I know you love this woman, Bri. Hang in there. I'm just sorry I couldn't do more. Good luck."

Chapter 18

Jennifer woke in yet another strange place. It was hot, dark, and she could hear women's voices whispering. "What is this?"

"Are you American?" A voice in the dark sounded eager. "Yes. Where are we?"

"We're in a shipping container, on a boat to Odessa where we're going to be –"

She broke down into soft sobbing. "We're going to be sold."

"Where are the guards?" Jennifer tried to focus in the dark. "How many of us are in here?"

"The guards are outside, walking around the deck. There are seven of us."

Jennifer wiped the sweat dripping from her forehead. "What's your name?"

"I'm Becky. I was doing my sophomore year abroad and the best I can figure is my host family sold me. A man showed up at their house, paid them a big wad of money and then took me. I tried to fight, but I think he broke one of my ribs."

"Does anybody else speak English?"

"I do" said a little voice at the far end of the container. "I was promised a job as a nanny, and they took my passport."

Jennifer had read enough about human trafficking to know there was usually a plant, someone pretending to be a captive to keep an eye on things from the inside. Light finally began peeking in through a crack.

Must be dawn.

She looked around at the faces in the hot, cramped metal box.
Who could it be?

A pretty, but ragged, blonde smiled meekly. "Hi."

Jennifer recognized the voice as the Becky she'd been talking to.

Steel scraped, and the door of the container opened. An armed man handed his rifle off to his partner at the door and walked in.

He looked around the container at all the women and then grabbed Becky by the hair and threw her into the middle of the small metal room.

She wimpered. "No, no. Please?"

He slapped her across the face so hard her head hit the floor. It was a power play, to beat one of them in front of all the others would break their spirits and make certain they were absolutely clear as to who was in charge.

Jennifer scrambled over to the girl. "Becky? Becky, look at me," Jennifer whispered. "Focus on me. We'll get through this."

Tears streamed down Becky's cheeks. "I want to die. Let me die."

The man stood over Becky and backhanded Jennifer. "Get away from her. You're next!"

A storm swelled inside Jennifer. Her fears of her own experience had held her captive for too long. If she made a move, the man's partner would probably kill her.

No, I will not be a victim any longer, nor will any of these girls.

Anger boiled, and rage exploded as Jennifer launched herself onto the man and punched at his face in blind rage. Blood sprayed from his lips and nose. Her hands were red with it. She could taste it on her lips. She kept punching.

Someone pulled her off the man but she kept fighting.

If I'm about to die, I'm going out swinging.

She squinted against the sun now streaming in and saw the crimson blood on her hands. A familiar voice spoke in soothing tones. She shook her head and blinked her way back to reality.

Someone else was there. "Jason?"

"Hey, flare gun." He checked the man's neck for a pulse and shook his head. "You done good. You're safe now." He smiled wide.

Whoever had grabbed her had loosened their grip. "I couldn't let him. I couldn't let him make her a victim." She sobbed and turned away, toward the person who'd pulled her off the man.

Can it be?

"Brian?"

~~~

He pulled her close. "It's okay. You survived. You're safe now."

Jason checked his watch. "Bri, this heap is going to pull into port soon. We need to extract these girls now."

Brian looked at each woman. They were all the worse for wear, staring through swollen eyes. He motioned for them to get up. "Can you all walk?"

Jason did a silent head count as the women stood up. "I count eight people here. Our little boat won't hold more than ten."

"We'll figure it out. Let's get these women out of this can." He motioned for the women to come out.

Jason shook his head. "There's gonna be an international incident, reprimands, and we'll probably lose our jobs."

A pretty Asian girl cried out. "I can't go home after this. The shame."

Jason spoke softly to her as he helped her to her feet. "It's okay, hon. Who do you want to be? I know a guy in Morocco who can give you a whole new life."

"No, please don't sell me!"

"No, no." He shook his head. "He'll create papers for you. You can be anyone you want to be, anywhere in the world. Maybe go somewhere nice to recuperate before going home. How about Italy?

We've got a friend with a place there. She can help you build a new life."

"But how?"

Jason helped another woman up and walked toward Brian. "She's got a soft spot for women who need a fresh..." Jason trailed off as a woman insinuated herself between him and Brian, pointing the muzzle of a Glock at Brian's head.

"Move over there with the women." She sounded convinced she was in control.

Not on your fucking life, bitch.

Brian smiled. "And the hits just keep on coming, eh, Jase?"

Catch the reference, bro.

Jason slowly cracked his knuckles. "What I can't figure is if this is a cross or just a straight up knockout?"

"Shut up and move!" The woman with the gun had likely been planted by the slavers to keep the women scared and under control.

Brian moved Jennifer toward the other women and winked at her. "You call it, Jason."

"I said, move over there!" She didn't sound as in control now.

Jason raised his hands to shoulder height slowly. "Sure, whatever you say." In a single move, he spun all of his significant weight into a right cross to the throat that knocked the woman out.

She dropped like a wet rag and the gun fell to the deck.

Jason grabbed the gun and turned back around smiling his Cheshire cat grin. "That bitch was crazy. Good news is, we just freed up some space on the boat."

"Nice cross, brother. Let's go, ladies!"

Chapter 19

Brian watched Jennifer sit down in the private jet and breathe deep. Within an hour, she'd gone from being a prisoner in a cargo box to flying in a private jet. She was handling it like a champ.

Brian sat down and held her hand. "I'll bet you're anxious to get home and relax a little, huh?"

"Thank you for all this." She squeezed his hand. "But I'm already behind schedule by...I don't even know how many days."

"What do you mean?"

"I still have to get a crew together. I have work to do in Algeria. There are investors I have to answer to, and more importantly, a wreck I really want to find."

Jason shook his head and chuckled. "Like a dog with a bone."

"How did you find me, anyway?"

Jason's phone rang and he looked at the screen. "Speak of the devil." He answered and held the phone to his ear. "Good morning, sir!" He nodded to Brian. "On our way back to Morocco now. Yeah, she's here. Just a minute." He handed the phone to Jennifer. "For you, Flare Gun."

Jennifer looked askance at Jason and took the phone. "Hello?..." She scowled, "Agent? You sent him?" She eyed Brian and her voice turned cold. "I won't pass a drug test for a while, but yes, I'm okay...Did you say Agent?" She glared over at Brian and then at Jason.

Jason smiled his Cheshire cat grin but it soon fell.

Brian watched as her expression changed in an instant. Like a Texas storm, she was about to blow.

"You had spies posted on me!? You posted babysitters on me! You even had one pretend to date me? How could you, Papa?"

Brian leaned back in his seat and tipped his head back to the headrest.

Thank God I have her on a plane. It's gonna take some time to work through that temper and explain all of this.

Jason grinned and tapped Brian on the knee. "Flare gun time." The sparkle in his eyes was unmistakable.

Brian shook his head at Jason and mouthed the word "No".

He's not wrong.

"He what?" She looked quizzically at Brian. "I'll be the judge of that." Jennifer paused. "I'll call you when we get back." She handed the phone back to Jason and glared at them both. "Where were you when my father called?"

Jason jumped in, ready to tell the story. "I was on the Zodiac, getting dressed. Brian took the call."

"Getting dressed?" Jennifer raised her hand for him to stop. "My questions will be directed at Brian until such time as I say otherwise."

Jason smiled and shook his head. "I like you Flare gun! Carry on."

"Where were you?"

Brian took a deep breath and exhaled. This was going differently than he'd hoped. "When I received your call, I had Chris start satellite tracking, and rousted Jason for backup. We went to your boat where I investigated the scene. Jason had eyes on your kidnappers' boat so we were about to prep your boat to follow when your father called."

Jennifer still wasn't sold. "He called you?"

Brian shook his head. "No, he called you on your phone. I saw the photo and caller ID and that's when I knew he was your father."

"And that's when he got involved?" She asked.

"Not really." Brian winced. "I made him jump through some hoops to contact me through official channels so I could get on with finding you before the red tape began."

Did she just almost smile?

"You barely knew me. Why would you leave the mission you were on?"

"Call me a sucker. I fell in love with a woman who turned me down so I followed her by boat, swam onto unfriendly foreign soil, stole a car, wrecked the car, ran a few klicks, redirected money from a black budget, posed as a human trafficker, called in some favors from the Russian mob, hijacked a cargo ship and hoped it would win her over."

She looked over at Jason. "And you? Why would you participate?"

Jason's eyes opened wide. "Me?" He pointed to himself. "Well, let's see…"

"Jason, just answer the question honestly." Brian groaned.

"Well, you see, I've known Brian for a very long time and he has never been in love. Frankly, he was a bit of a slut."

Brian rubbed his forehead. "Not helping, Jase."

"Hold on. I'm getting there. He fell head over heels for you at first sight. When you spent all that time together but hadn't, you know, I knew it was serious." Jason thought for a moment. "Okay, so Brian wakes me one morning for bullets before breakfast and I'm always down for that so I grab my clothes and fire up the Zodiac. Then he says it's you--and I can't have the future mother of my nieces and nephews just get taken, so here I am."

"Okay, that's enough. This isn't helping, Jason." Brian stood and turned to Jennifer, offering his hand. "Can we please go in the back and talk? You could probably use some rest anyway."

When they reached the cabin, Brian opened the door and let Jennifer enter first. "Jason's my brother and a great guy, but investigators hate him and you may be a bit tired for wrangling a straight answer out of him. Here are the facts: I did fall in love with you, I went against orders to find you, and luckily it all worked out in the end. You made your feelings clear and I respect that. I have no expectations—"

"Brian, shut up." Jennifer snaked her arms around his neck and kissed him softly. "When you said you loved me, it broke my heart to turn you away but my father...his job...my job...well, it was just too complicated."

Brian held her close and smiled down at her. "Still complicated?"

She kissed his cheek. "It's all very simple now." She paused and looked into his eyes. "I love you too."

Brian smiled, took a deep breath and exhaled. "Now that's settled, can we please travel together from now on?"

Jennifer pulled away to arm's length. "I'm not joining the Agency."

"Well, that's a relief because I'm not staying." Brian pulled her close again.

"You aren't?"

"Nope." He pulled the gold coin from his pocket and handed it to her. "I've found my treasure. Let's go find yours."

About the Author

Lisa Pietsch (pen name of Lisa Woodward) is the Publishing Director at Defiance Press and Publishing, an Air Force Veteran, former magazine publisher, multi-published author, mother of two giants, and wife to a Viking.

Lisa speaks French, Spanish, Norwegian, and Russian. She has been USAF Security Forces Leader, received specialized training as an FBI Hostage Negotiator, and worked with MI-5 on personal security details for both British and Jordanian Royals. These diverse experiences inspire her Task Force 125 series, which follows Sarah Stevens, a CIA Special Activities Division recruit, through gripping tales of espionage and paramilitary operations.

In 2020, Lisa's life took a romantic turn when she reconnected with the love of her life, the man who inspired her Task Force 125 series, launching her into her greatest adventure yet.

An avid gamer, Lisa enjoys both console and tabletop gaming, where she goes by "Geniekin" on Xbox and Roll20.

As Lisa Pietsch, she crafts thrilling paramilitary action/adventure/romance novels, while as Lisa Woodward, she weaves enchanting epic romantic fantasy tales.